聽新多益
第一次就拿
閱讀高分

力得文化編輯群◎著

極速秒搶閱讀高分！

Tune into the Language of Your Intuition

MP3

New TOEIC閱讀搶分 『**速度**』是絕對關鍵

提升解題速度 快還要更快 『**鮮活語感**』才是主道

學習步驟

➤ **10**組核心題型：將新多益Part 5考題以職場工作類型分類

快速掌握新多益題型及相關字彙

閱讀高分 ☑ Get

➤ **3**大學習要點：精選新多益Part 5 擬真考題＋精闢的文法解析＋超語感聽力練習

將考題迅速融會貫通 打造超強英語耳

閱讀高分 ☑ Get

附MP3 － 專業外籍老師錄製、清晰女聲、閱讀及聽力同步訓練

編者序

新多益要拿高分，關鍵在於「速度」，尤其是在 Part 5、6、7 的部分，短短的 75 分鐘內要完成 100 道的題目，對於許多非英語母語人士而言，是一項極大的挑戰！

坊間常見的方式，是以文法來作為新多益題型中最主要的解題方式，但這樣的分析方式，除非是對於文法概念相當熟稔，否則是極有可能會因此而耽誤到解題的速度。

本書精選 Part 5 題型中的 300 道考題，以工作類型的分類，除了有題目的文法解析之外，還加上了 MP3。讓讀者能邊讀邊聽，以『聽』的方式，熟悉新多益的題型，鮮活讀者的語感。希望能幫助讀者都能在最短的時間內在新多益閱讀題上有最亮眼的表現！

力得文化編輯群

目次 CONTENTS

擬真試題

1. Please be aware that all personal - - - - - - - - sent from the office computers is subject to review by the management staff.

(A) corresponding
(B) correspondingly
(C) correspondent
(D) correspondence

中譯 (D) 請注意所有從辦公室電腦所寄出的個人書信皆需受管理階層的審查。

解析 本題考題屬於『名詞』的考法。判斷上下文後優先選『靜態名詞』，亦即不用動作（主、被動）含意的名詞，選項 (A) 先排除，所以選擇 (D)。(B) 選項為副詞，與文法不符，所以不選。(C) 選項是動詞所變化而來的名詞，指的是「記者」，與上下句意不合，所以不選。

超語感練習 🎧 Track 001

Please be aware that all personal correspondence sent from the office computers is subject to review by the management staff.

2. - - - - - - - - who worked overtime on the weekend to finish the project were given Monday morning off as compensation.
(A) Them
(B) That
(C) Their
(D) Those

中譯 (D) 那些週末超時工作以完成計畫的員工，將給予星期一上午的補休。

解析 本題考題屬於『代名詞』當主詞的考法。句中主要子句動詞為複數動詞 were given，而主要子句主詞為代名詞主格用法，且需用複數形，故選擇 (D)。(A) 選項為代名詞受詞用法，與文法不符，所以不選。(B) 選項為代名詞主格用法，且為單數形，與文法不符，所以不選。

超語感練習  Track 002

Those who worked overtime on the weekend to finish the project were given Monday morning off as compensation.

3. When Ms. Huang found that the -------- system was out of order, she called the repairman in to look at it right away.

(A) secure

(B) security

(C) secured

(D) securing

中譯　(B) 當黃小姐發現負責安全的系統故障時，她立即打電話請維修人員過來檢修。

解析　本題考題屬於『名詞(片語)＋名詞』的考法。上下文應是指，這系統是屬於『負責「安全」』的系統，與動作（主、被動）、形容詞（內外在特質）無關，所以選擇(B)。

超語感練習　Track 003

When Ms. Huang found that the security system was out of order, she called the repairman in to look at it right away.

聽新多益 Part 5，第一次就拿閱讀高分

4. No sooner had he arrived at his home than he was called back to the office to deal with a matter of --------.
(A) urgency
(B) urge
(C) urging
(D) urgent

中譯 (A) 他一到家就被公司用電話召回處理這緊急事件。

解析 本題考題屬於『介系詞 (in) ＋名詞』的考法。因為是句子結尾處，所以判斷上下文後優先選『靜態名詞』，所以選擇 (A)。選項 (B) 是動詞，且在一個句子中沒有做適當的變化，與文法不符，所以不選。(C) 選項是動詞所變化而來的形式，判斷上下文後並無需要動作（主動）含意的名詞句意，所以不選。(D) 選項是動詞所變化而來的形容詞，與文法用法不符，所以不選。

超語感練習  Track 004

No sooner had he arrived at his home than he was called back to the office to deal with a matter of urgency.

5. I have talked with him about being late for the office twice already, but it hasn't made much of an - - - - - - - - on him.

(A) impressing
(B) impression
(C) impressive
(D) impress

中譯 **(B)** 我已經跟他提及他 2 次上班遲到的事情，但這對他好像沒啥印象。

解析 本題考題屬於『冠詞』的考法。冠詞 (a/an)＋單數名詞的應用。且應用『靜態名詞』，與動作（主、被動）無關，且後面有相搭配名詞用法的介系詞 (on) 出現，所以選擇 (B)。(C) 選項是動詞所變化而來的形式 (-sive)，為形容詞用法，與前後用法不符，所以不選。(D) 選項是動詞 impress，且在一個句子中沒有做適當的變化，與文法不符，所以不選。

超語感練習 🎧 Track 005

I have talked with him about being late for the office twice already, but it hasn't made much of an impression on him.

6. Nitche Stationery sells a variety of office supplies, and many ------- office appliances for nearly a decade, and has been very satisfied with our quality.

(A) the other
(B) another
(C) others
(D) other

中譯 (D) 尼采文具這公司販售各種辦公室用品,還有許多其他的辦公室器具將近 10 年的時間,一直以來也十分滿意我們的品質。

解析 本題考題屬於『代名詞』的考法。由上下文判斷,應該選「其他的」這個中文,所以為形容詞用法,所以答案選擇 (D)。選項 (A) 可以是代名詞或形容詞用法,因為與文法衝突,所以不選。(B) 選項可以是代名詞或形容詞用法,與文法衝突,所以不選。(C) 選項是 others 這個字做代名詞的用法,且是複數形式,也因為與本句題目衝突,直接不考慮。

超語感練習  Track 006

Nitche Stationery sells a variety of office supplies, and many other office appliances for nearly a decade, and has been very satisfied with our quality.

7. Though a final decision has not yet to be made, the company has tentatively decided to hold the office staff training session on -------- of March.

(A) four

(B) the four

(C) fourth

(D) the fourth

中譯 (D) 雖然最後結論未產生，公司暫時將員工訓練時段定在 3 月 4 日。

解析 本題考題屬於代名詞考法中，『序數』的考法。表示日期應當用序數表示，且應該用定冠詞 (the) ＋序數加以配合，所以選擇 (D)。選項 (A) 為數字，與文法用法不符，所以不選。(B) 選項為 the ＋數字，與文法用法不符，所以不選。(C) 選項雖然為序數，但前面沒有 the，與文法用法不符，所以不選。

超語感練習 Track 007

Though a final decision has not yet to be made, the company has tentatively decided to hold the office staff training session on the fourth of March.

8. Office commuters can help reduce pollution by occasionally leaving - - - - - - - - cars at home and using public transportation.
   (A) them
   (B) their
   (C) theirs
   (D) they

中譯　(B) 辦公室通勤族偶爾把他們的車留在家中,並使用大眾運輸工具的方式,能幫忙降低汙染。

解析　本題考題屬於代名詞考法。名詞前面接『代名詞的所有格』用法,所以選擇 (B)。(A) 選項是代名詞的受詞用法,與文法用法不符,所以不選。(C) 選項是所有格的代名詞用法,後面不應該再有名詞,與文法用法不符,所以不選。(D) 選項是所有格的主詞用法,與用法不符,所以不選。

超語感練習　Track 008

Office commuters can help reduce pollution by occasionally leaving their cars at home and using public transportation.

9. In recognition of Elaine Tang's exceptional service to
-------- company, the human resources director will honor
her at tonight's employee awards ceremony.

(A) ours
(B) our
(C) us
(D) we

中譯 **(B)** 為了表彰 Elaine Tang 對我們公司的卓越貢獻,人力資源主管將在
今晚員工頒獎典禮上表彰她。

解析 本題考題屬於『代名詞所有格』的用法,所以用代名詞的所有格用法,
所以選擇 (B)。(A) 選項是所有格的代名詞用法,是所有格與代名詞合併
的結果,後面不應再有名詞,與文法用法不符,所以不選。(C) 選項是
代名詞的受詞用法,與文法用法不符,所以不選。(D) 選項是代名詞的
主詞用法,與文法用法不符,所以不選。

超語感練習 🎧 Track 009

In recognition of Elaine Tang's exceptional service
to our company, the human resources director will
honor her at tonight's employee awards ceremony.

10. - - - - - - - - invest heavily in research, find creative solutions to problems, and plan down to the last detail.
(A) They
(B) Theirs
(C) Them
(D) Themselves

中譯　(A) 那些人／公司／機構投資許多在研究上、找出問題的有創意性的解答、及規劃詳細細節。

解析　本題考題屬於『代名詞』當主詞的考法，與對等連接詞相搭配的文法概念考法。and 為對等連接詞，連接前後詞性相等的結構（動詞 invest, find and plan），且句中動詞為複數動詞型態，所以判斷上下文後優先選複數形名詞，故選擇 (A)。(B) 選項為所有格的代名詞用法，句意與上下文不符，所以不選。(C) 選項為代名詞的受詞用法，與文法不符，所以不選。(D) 選項為代名詞的反身代名詞用法，與文法不符，所以不選。

超語感練習 Track 010

They invest heavily in research, find creative solutions to problems, and plan down to the last detail.

11. International experience is the main - - - - - - - - that separates Mr. Sloan from the other candidates for the position.

(A) qualified

(B) qualification

(C) qualify

(D) qualifying

中譯 **(B)** Sloan 先生所具備的國際經驗，是區分他與其他職位申請候選人的主要資格。

解析 本題考題屬於『形容詞＋名詞』的考法。上下文並不需要有動作（主動）含意的名詞，也不需要帶有動作（主動 / 進行）含意的形容詞或副詞，所以不選 (A)、(D)；所以選『靜態名詞』表示「結果」字尾變化的 -tion 選項 (B)。(C) 選項是動詞，且在一個句子中沒有做適當的變化，與文法用法不符，所以不選。

超語感練習 🎧 Track 011

International experience is the main qualification that separates Mr. Sloan from the other candidates for the position.

12. Improvements in the manufacturing process resulted in greater - - - - - - - - in the production of wood furniture.
(A) consistency
(B) consisting
(C) consistently
(D) consistent

中譯 (A) 改善製造過程能帶來木製家具生產的一致性。

解析 本題考題屬於『介系詞＋名詞』的考法。介系詞後面需接『靜態名詞』或『動名詞』。而動名詞本身帶有動作特質，後面應有接受動作的受詞；但空格後為另一個介系詞片語，不見受詞。所以不選 (B)，而選擇『靜態名詞』(A)。(C) 選項是副詞，與文法不符，所以不選。(D) 選項是形容詞，句意與上下文不符，所以不選。

超語感練習  Track 012

Improvements in the manufacturing process resulted in greater consistency in the production of wood furniture.

13. Costs for office building materials, such as cement, steel, and wood, rose sharply last quarter, lowering the - - - - - - - - of most construction companies.

(A) profiting
(B) profitable
(C) profit
(D) profits

中譯 (D) 建造辦公室大樓的建材的成本，比如水泥、鋼鐵與木頭，在上一季急遽地上升，而這些降低了大多數建材公司的利潤。

解析 本題考題屬於『名詞』的考法。與動作（主、被動）無關，不考慮 (A)。(B) 選項為形容詞用法，中文翻譯為「可獲利的」，與題目要求的文法不符，所以不選。(C) 選項在上下文中，因為前面的名詞「成本」costs 為複數，則之後的「獲利／利潤」應為 profits，也就是前後名詞應都要使用名詞複數，以達前後一致，所以選 (D)。

超語感練習 Track 013

Costs for office building materials, such as cement, steel, and wood, rose sharply last quarter, lowering the profits of most construction companies.

14. Basic charges for your monthly office telephone service are billed 15 days in - - - - - - - - at the end of each month.

(A) advance
(B) advanced
(C) advancement
(D) advancing

中譯 (A) 每月辦公室的基本電話費，會事先在每月月底 15 天前結算。

解析 本題考題屬於『介系詞＋名詞』的考法。空格不見受詞。所以判斷上下文後，與動作（主、被動）無關，不考慮 (B)、(D)，而選擇『靜態名詞』(A)。(C) 選項中文是「前進、進步」，句意與上下文不符，所以不選。

超語感練習 Track 014

Basic charges for your monthly office telephone service are billed 15 days in advance at the end of each month.

15. The rising - - - - - - - - of an upturn in the economy means we feel that now is the time for the company to embark on a campaign of rapid expansion.

(A) expected
(B) expectation
(C) expectancy
(D) expecting

中譯 (B) 愈是期待經濟好轉，就愈表示我們認為公司快速擴展的時機就是現在。

解析 本題考題屬於『形容詞＋名詞』的考法。空格後為另一個介系詞片語，不見受詞。所以判斷上下文後，優先選擇『靜態名詞』，所以不選 (A)、(D)。(C) 選項是名詞，中文翻譯為「期望之事物」。expectancy 的英英定義為："the feeling or hope that something exciting, interesting, or good is about to happen"。 而 expectation 的英英定義為："hope of gaining sth/that sth will happen"。上下文中 "期望經濟好轉" 應當是從不景氣開始，逐漸期待或預期的好轉，與 expectancy 那種原本歡欣愉悅的意思有落差，所以選 (B)。

超語感練習 🎧 Track 015

The rising expectation of an upturn in the economy means we feel that now is the time for the company to embark on a campaign of rapid expansion.

16. In order to maintain - - - - - - - - within the department, we
have decided to appoint the new manager from inside the
company instead of looking for a completely new face.
(A) continuity
(B) continued
(C) continuous
(D) continuing

中譯 (A) 為了要維持部門內運作的連續性，我們必須決定從內部指派一位新
的經理，而不是去尋求一位新面孔（不熟悉公司事務的人）。

解析 本題考題屬於『名詞』考法中，『靜態名詞』或『動名詞』的考法。這
裡空格後為另一個介系詞片語，並沒有受詞存在，所以判斷上下文後，
優先選擇『靜態名詞』的答案，所以選 (A)。選項 (B)、(D) 是動詞演變
而來的用法，句意與上下文不符，所以不選。(C) 選項是形容詞用法，
與文法用法不符，所以不選。

超語感練習 🎧 Track 016

In order to maintain continuity within the
department, we have decided to appoint the new
manager from inside the company instead of
looking for a completely new face.

17. Our firm spokesman is pleased to announce that despite our lower expectations in employee - - - - - - - at the recent technology exhibition, the number was in fact higher than that in previous years.

(A) attended
(B) attendance
(C) attendants
(D) attending

中譯 (B) 我們公司的發言人高興地宣布，儘管員工在最近科技展的出席人數不如預期，然而出席人數事實上比前幾年要高出許多。

解析 本題考題屬於『名詞 (片語) ＋名詞』的考法。名詞 (片語) 組用來修飾後面名詞時，通常表示後面名詞的『功能』、『種類』、『材質』、『位置』。上下文應是指，這是屬於『員工的「出席」』，與動作 (主、被動) 無關，所以不選 (A)、(D)，選擇 (B)。(C) 選項是「與會人員」，與句意不符，所以不選。

超語感練習 🎧 Track 017

Our firm spokesman is pleased to announce that despite our lower expectations in employee attendance at the recent technology exhibition, the number was in fact higher than that in previous years.

18. According to the conditions that were agreed upon prior to the project, I'm afraid that the completion date is not really for mutual - - - - - - - -.

(A) negotiate
(B) negotiating
(C) negotiation
(D) negotiated

中譯 (C) 根據這計畫之前所同意的條約內容，雙方恐怕無法進行協商，共同決定完工日期。

解析 本題考題屬於『介系詞 (for) ＋名詞』的考法。空格前面雖然有形容詞，但真正結構是介系詞 (for) ＋名詞的介系詞片語。空格後面並無受詞，所以優先選『靜態名詞』(C)。選項 (A) 是動詞，且在一個句子中沒有做適當的變化，與文法用法不符。(B)、(D) 選項是動詞所變化而來的形式，與文法用法不符，所以不考慮。

超語感練習 Track 018

According to the conditions that were agreed upon prior to the project, I'm afraid that the completion date is not really for mutual negotiation.

19. It is important to remember that you pay absolutely nothing until you are actually in - - - - - - - - of the goods.

(A) reception
(B) receive
(C) receiving
(D) received

中譯　(A) 要記住，重要的是在你確切收到物品之前，你是絕對不用付出任何款項的。

解析　本題考題屬於『介系詞 (in) ＋名詞』的考法。空格後面沒有受詞，所以優先選『靜態名詞』(A)，不用動作 (主、被動) 含意的詞性 (C)、(D)。(B) 選項是動詞，且在一個句子中沒有做適當的變化，與文法用法不符，直接不考慮。

超語感練習　🎧 Track 019

It is important to remember that you pay absolutely nothing until you are actually in reception of the goods.

20. The office assistant provides administrative - - - - - - - to the staff of the Sales and Marketing Department.

(A) supportive
(B) support
(C) supporting
(D) supported

中譯 (B) 辦公室的助理將行政支援提供給銷售與行銷部門的職員。

解析 本題考題屬於『靜態名詞』或『動名詞』的考法。空格後面沒有受詞，所以優先選『靜態名詞』，與動作（主、被動）無關，不考慮(C)、(D)，所以選(B)。選項(A)是形容詞用法，用來修飾『名詞的內外在狀態』，與文法用法不符，所以不選。

超語感練習 🎧 Track 020

The office assistant provides administrative support to the staff of the Sales and Marketing Department.

21. I was glad - - - - - - - - my former manager again after so many years at a rival company.
(A) see
(B) to see
(C) seeing
(D) saw

中譯 (B) 我開心在那麼多年後，在競爭對手公司再次見到我的前任經理。

解析 不定詞做形容詞補語，to see「見到」，修飾 glad「開心」。主詞是人的時候，形容詞是一種情緒，主詞 I「我」，glad「開心」形容詞（一種情緒），故選 (B)。例句：We are happy to have you here.（我們高興有你在這裡。）

超語感練習　Track 021

I was glad to see my former manager again after so many years at a rival company.

22. The assistant - - - - - - - we employed last month is to be offered a new permanent position in another department.
(A) which
(B) that
(C) where
(D) what

中譯 **(B)** 我們去年雇用的助理，上個月另一個部門提供她新的永久職位。

解析 關係代名詞 who 或 that 都可用來引導形容詞子句，代表在它前面的人。選項 (A)、(C) 皆為關係代名詞，但各代表它前面的東西和地方。選項 (D)，不是關係代名詞。例句：The boy that my son is talking to is Jim. 我兒子正跟在他說話的那個男孩是 Jim。

超語感練習 Track 022

The assistant that we employed last month is to be offered a new permanent position in another department.

23. Rita Palmer, a new secretary, has succeeded in - - - - - - - - almost everyone in the office with her continuous gossiping.

(A) upset
(B) to upset
(C) upsettingly
(D) upsetting

中譯　(D) Rita Palmer，新來的祕書，隨著她持續的傳播流言蜚語，成功地讓幾乎每位在辦公室裡的人心煩。

解析　"succeed in"，in 是介系詞，所以後面要用名詞。選項 (A) 是動詞、選項 (B) 是不定詞，而選項 (C) 是副詞，選項 (D) 是 Ving 為動名詞，故選 (D)。

超語感練習　🎧 Track 023

Rita Palmer, a new secretary, has succeeded in upsetting almost everyone in the office with her continuous gossiping.

24. The warning to the lower management about the lax style of management was delivered by the company vice president --------.

(A) force
(B) forceful
(C) forcefully
(D) forcefulness

中譯 (C) 對於基層其鬆散風格管理方式的告誡,是由公司的副總裁十分強而有力地傳達。

解析 選項 (A) 為動詞,選項 (B) 為形容詞,選項 (D) 是名詞。本題是以副詞修飾過去分詞做形容詞的 delivered「傳達」,故選 (C)。

超語感練習  Track 024

The warning to the lower management about the lax style of management was delivered by the company vice president forcefully.

25. The points - - - - - - - - at the shareholders' annual meeting were too important to be disregarded without further discussion.

(A) elevated
(B) raised
(C) lifted
(D) risen

中譯 **(B)** 在股東年度會議提出的問題太過重要，無法在沒有進一步談論的狀況下漠視。

解析 會議中提出的問題，為過去式，需選擇過去式動詞。而選項 (A)(B)(C)(D) 均有升起之意，但選項 (D) 為過去分詞，rise「上升」的動詞三態為 rise–rose –risen，故刪去。而因題意需選擇有「提出」之意，故選擇 (B) 選項。

超語感練習 Track 025

The points raised at the shareholders' annual meeting were too important to be disregarded without further discussion.

26. The after dinner comments made by the company chairman were greatly - - - - - - - - by all employees.

(A) appreciate
(B) appreciated
(C) appreciating
(D) to appreciate

中譯 (B) 晚餐過後公司主席做的評語，十分受到所有員工讚賞。

解析 選項 (A) 為原形動詞，選項 (B) 為過去式或過去分詞，選項 (C) 是動名詞，選項 (D) 為不定詞。而依題意為過去式被動語態，主詞＋was/were＋過去分詞，故選 (B)。

超語感練習  **Track 026**

The after dinner comments made by the company chairman were greatly appreciated by all employees.

27. Global Inc. announces the - - - - - - - - of George Raymond as its new CEO with immediate effect.

(A) engagement
(B) appointment
(C) introduction
(D) authorization

中譯 (B) 全國股份有限公司宣佈任命 George Raymond 為新任執行長且即刻生效。

解析 選項 (A) 為訂婚；選項 (B) 為任命、派任；選項 (C) 為介紹；選項 (D) 為授權。依照題意，選擇 (B)。

超語感練習 Track 027

Global Inc. announces the appointment of George Raymond as its new CEO with immediate effect.

28. The announcement said that all assembly workers can stop
- - - - - - - - lunch at 12pm.

(A) to eat
(B) eating
(C) eat
(D) eaten

中譯　(A) 公告上說，所有組裝工人可以在中午 12 點停止工作去吃午餐。

解析　stop「停止」可以加不定詞或動名詞，但是意思不同。stop to eat 「停止某事然後去做另一件事」。stop eating「馬上停止做你現在正在 做的事」。

超語感練習　 Track 028

The announcement said that all assembly workers
can stop to eat lunch at 12pm.

29. Following the disorganized product launch either Mr. Peters or Mr. Abraham - - - - - - - expected to be fired, at the board meeting next week.

(A) are

(B) was

(C) is

(D) were

中譯　(C) 隨著無組織的產品發表，預計不是 Peters 先生就是 Abraham 先生，會在下週的董事會議被開除。

解析　"either… or"「不是……就是」，所以知道主詞為單數，所以須用 be 動詞 "is" 或 "was"，是現在式，故選 (C)。例句：Either Maya or Nancy was hit by a car last night.（不是 Maya 就是 Nancy 昨晚被車撞。）

超語感練習　🎧 Track 029

Following the disorganized product launch either Mr. Peters or Mr. Abraham is expected to be fired, at the board meeting next week.

30. Any - - - - - - - behavior towards our employees will not be tolerated and will be immediately reported to the police.

(A) threat
(B) threatening
(C) threaten
(D) threatened

中譯　(B) 任何對我們員工脅迫的行為，將不會被容忍並且會立刻報警處理。

解析　選項 (A) 為動詞、選項 (B) 為形容詞、選項 (C) 為動詞，選項 (D) 為形容詞。問題中 behavior 為名詞，前面應加形容詞做修飾，而選項 (D) 為「受到威脅的」。以題意須選擇 B，「脅迫的」最為恰當。

超語感練習　 Track 030

Any threatening behavior towards our employees will not be tolerated and will be immediately reported to the police.

擬真試題

1. A monthly newsletter highlighting the achievements of the company will especially be sent out to keep the newcomers better - - - - - - - - as well as positive on duty.
   (A) informative
   (B) information
   (C) informed
   (D) informing

中譯 (C) 強調公司成就的每月通訊將會特別發送給那些新進人員，讓他們持續被妥善告知，並在工作時保持正面態度。

解析 這是『使役動詞 (keep)』的考法。keep 的對象為新進人員 (newcomers)，inform 用來修飾受詞 (newcomers)；但是後面並未有受詞，所以用被動的『動態形容詞』，中文解釋為「被告知的」，所以去除 (B) 選擇 (C)。選項 (A) 是『靜態形容詞』，英英解釋為 "sb./sth. providing a lot of useful information"，「資訊的主動提供者」，與句意不符，所以不選。選項 (D) 是 V-ing『動態形容詞』，中文解釋為「（主動）告知的」，不符句意所以不選。

超語感練習 🎧 Track 031

A monthly newsletter highlighting the achievements of the company will especially be sent out to keep the newcomers better informed as well as positive on duty.

Unit 1
Unit 2
Unit 3
Unit 4
Unit 5
Unit 6
Unit 7
Unit 8
Unit 9
Unit 10

2. Though the company considers the orientation is the most efficient method in adjusting rookies to our firm in the very short time, many people find the intensive training schedule rather - - - - - - - -.

(A) exhausting
(B) exhausted
(C) exhaustingly
(D) exhaustion

中譯 (A) 雖然公司認為，新生員工訓練是在很短的時間調整新秀、讓他們適應我們公司最有效的方法，但很多人發現，密集的訓練日程是相當累人的。

解析 本題考題屬於『認為 (find)』的考法。從上下文得知，find 的主詞為人 (poeple)，相搭配的動詞選項為 exhaust，可以為『情緒動詞』使用。上下文的句意中，既是指他人的價值判斷，應當用現在分詞 (V-ing) 用法，所以答案選 (A)，不選 (B)。選項 (C) 是副詞用法，選項 (D) 是名詞用法，與上下文不符，所以不選。

超語感練習  Track 032

Though the company considers the orientation is the most efficient method in adjusting rookies to our firm in the very short time, many people find the intensive training schedule rather exhausting.

3. Starting from next week, headquarters will have entrance permits - - - - - - - - for the use of recruiting employees in the fair.

(A) issue
(B) issues
(C) issuing
(D) issued

中譯 (D) 從下週起，總部會發出進出許可證，給在商展招募員工的職員所使用。

解析 本題考題屬於『使役動詞 (have)』的考法。從上下文得知，have 的對象為非人的名詞 (permits) 時，issue 應該用「被動 / 完成」行為的過去分詞 (V-p.p.)，中文解釋為「被發行的」用來修飾受詞 (permits)，所以選擇答案 (D)。選項 (B) 是名詞複數用法，所以不選。選項 (A) 是名詞單數用法或動詞原形用法，與上下文句意不符，所以不選。選項 (C) 是 V-ing 的主動『動態形容詞』，所以不選。

超語感練習 🎧 Track 033

Starting from next week, headquarters will have entrance permits issued for the use of recruiting employees in the fair.

4. Many job opportunities made recent graduates from the community college's business program - - - - - - - -, for the job fair held by the city government.

(A) appreciating
(B) appreciate
(C) appreciated
(D) to appreciate

中譯 (C) 近來諸多的工作機會，讓社區學院商業計劃畢業的應屆畢業生相當感謝市政府所舉辦的就業博覽會。

解析 本題考題屬於『使役動詞 (make)』的考法。從上下文得知，make 的驅使對象為名詞 (graduates) 時，appreciate 用來修飾受詞 (graduates)，且對象是人，應該用形容詞的過去分詞 (V-p.p.)，中文翻成「心懷感激的」，而不是選項 (A) 代表「主動 / 進行」行為的現在分詞 (V-ing)，中文翻成「令人感激的」。所以選擇答案 (C)。選項 (B) 是動詞原形用法，且在一個句子中沒有做適當的變化，與文法不符，所以不選。選項 (D) 是『不定詞』，與文法不符，所以不選。

超語感練習 **Track 034**

Many job opportunities made recent graduates from the community college's business program appreciated, for the job fair held by the city government.

5. Many workers were left - - - - - - - - when the company's production facility was shut down due to budget shortfalls.

(A) unemploy
(B) unemploying
(C) unemployment
(D) unemployed

中譯 (D) 由於預算短缺，該公司的生產設施被迫關閉，留下許多工人失業。

解析 本題考題屬於『使役動詞 (leave)』的考法。從上下文得知，leave 的驅使對象為名詞 (workers) 時，unemployed 用來修飾受詞 (workers)，且對象是人（員工），而且應當是被雇用的對象，應該用形容詞的過去分詞 (V-p.p.)，表示動作是因外力所導致的結果；中文翻成「不被雇用的」，與上下文句意符合，所以選擇答案 (D)。選項 (A) 是動詞原形用法，與文法不符，所以不選。選項 (B) 與上下文的句意不符，所以不選。選項 (C) 是名詞用法，與文法不符，所以不選。

超語感練習 🎧 Track 035

Many workers were left unemployed when the company's production facility was shut down due to budget shortfalls.

6. The Avery Career Center offers advice and assistance to get staff - - - - - - - - in non-technical professions to further ensure their job positions.

(A) acquirement
(B) acquiring
(C) acquired
(D) to acquire

中譯 (C) Avery 就業指導中心提供諮詢和協助，讓員工學會非技術的專業，以進一步確保他們的工作職位。

解析 本題考題屬於『使役動詞 (get)』的考法。從上下文得知，get 的驅使對象為名詞 (staff) 時，acquire 用來修飾受詞 (staff)。因為被驅使的動作 (acquire) 後面並沒有對象讓動作去執行，所以用形容詞的過去分詞 (V-p.p.) 表示「被動」，中文翻成「學習而來的」，而不是選項 (B) 表示「主動 / 進行」行為的現在分詞 (V-ing)，也不會是選項 (D) 代表不定詞的「主動、企圖、目的性」的用法。選項 (A) 是名詞，與上下文的句意不符，所以不選。

超語感練習  Track 036

The Avery Career Center offers advice and assistance to get staff acquired in non-technical professions to further ensure their job positions.

7. The firm is offering every branch a quota of fifty high quality complimentary gifts at competitive prices to make its product promotion - - - - - - - - nationwide.
   (A) successful
   (B) success
   (C) succeed
   (D) successfully

中譯　(A) 該公司以具競爭力的價格，提供每個分公司五十件高品質的贈品，讓它的產品促銷成功遍及全國。

解析　本題考題屬於『使役動詞(have)』的考法。使役動詞中，have 後面接形容詞來補充說明受詞的狀態，所以選擇答案(A)。選項(B)是名詞用法，句意明顯與上下文不符，所以不選。選項(C)是動詞；然而，這個句子的動詞(is offering)已經相當確定，並不需要動詞再出現，所以不選。選項(D)是副詞用法，句意明顯與上下文不符，所以不選。

超語感練習　🎧 Track 037

The firm is offering every branch a quota of fifty high quality complimentary gifts at competitive prices to make its product promotion successful nationwide.

8. Sitting through long presentations in staff orientation makes the newcomers - - - - - - -, so speakers should limit their talks to 30 minutes.

(A) rest
(B) restless
(C) to rest
(D) resting

中譯 (B) 在員工新進訓練時，長時間坐著聽長篇大論的演講，會讓新進人員無法休息；所以演講者應將談話限制在 30 分鐘內。

解析 本題考題屬於『使役動詞 (make)』的考法。上下文應該選無法休息，所以選 (B)。選項 (A) 無論是形容詞或動詞用法時，句意與上下文不符，所以不選。選項 (C) 是不定詞形式，與文法不符，所以不選。選項 (D) 是『動態形容詞』，句意與上下文不符，所以不選。

超語感練習 🎧 Track 038

Sitting through long presentations in staff orientation makes the newcomers restless, so speakers should limit their talks to 30 minutes.

9. If - - - - - - - - healthy is the main concern in choosing employees to our employers, then you should be prepared to choose someone watching what he/she eats and exercises regularly.

(A) making
(B) staying
(C) maintaining
(D) having

中譯 **(B)** 如果保持健康對雇主而言，是在選擇員工時主要關注的問題，那麼你應該準備，要從中選擇注意飲食與規律運動的人員。

解析 本題考題屬於『連綴動詞(stay)』的考法。「連綴動詞」後面必須接形容詞。四個選項中，只有答案(B)後面可以直接用形容詞。選項(A)是「使役動詞」，後面需接受詞後再接可能的動詞變化或形容詞用法，文法明顯與上下文不符，所以不選。選項(C)是「一般動詞」，後面需接受詞，與文法不符，所以不選。選項(D)是「使役動詞」或「一般動詞」用法時，後面需接受詞，與文法不符，所以不選。

超語感練習 Track 039

If staying healthy is the main concern in choosing employees to our employers, then you should be prepared to choose someone watching what he/she eats and exercises regularly.

10. Now, the Internet convenience has job seekers become
‑ ‑ ‑ ‑ ‑ ‑ ‑ ‑ to finding jobs on line and having their choices in
advance.
(A) accustoming
(B) accustomed
(C) accustom
(D) to accustom

中譯 (B) 現在，網路的便利已經讓求職者習慣於線上尋找工作，並提前加以
選擇。

解析 本題考題屬於『連綴動詞 (become)』的考法。連綴動詞後面必須接形
容詞，且該動詞 (accustom) 用法上應當用「被動」用法，所以選擇 (B)
「過去分詞 (V-p.p.)」用法來當作「形容詞」使用。選項 (A) 是 V-ing
現在分詞用法，與文法不符，所以不選。選項 (C) 是動詞用法時，然
而，這個句子的動詞 (is becoming) 已經相當確定，並不需要動詞再出
現，所以不選。選項 (D) 是不定詞，與文法不符，所以不選。

超語感練習 Track 040

Now, the Internet convenience has job seekers become
accustomed to finding jobs on line and having their
choices in advance.

11. Having notice emails for job hunters - - - - - - - - in advance without informing them isn't really an invasion of their privacy because they are only supposed to be informed by work-related mails from our office.

(A) to read
(B) reading
(C) read
(D) to reading

中譯 (C) 未告知求職者就由外部審查人員事先讀取發給他們的郵件，並不算是侵犯隱私，因為從我們辦公室發出給他們的信件，也僅止於和工作相關。

解析 本題考題屬於『使役動詞 (have)』的考法。使役動詞中，have 後面接動詞 (VR) 或形容詞來補充說明受詞的狀態，後面並未有執行被驅使動作的對象，所以應該用動詞所變化而來、代表「被動 / 完成」行為的過去分詞 (V-p.p.)，中文解釋為「被讀的」，所以選擇答案 (C)。選項 (A) 是不定詞，與文法不符，所以不選。選項 (B) 是現在分詞 (V-ing) 用法，表示主動行為，文法明顯與上下文不符，所以不選。選項 (D) 與文法不符，所以不選。

超語感練習 🎧 **Track 041**

Having notice emails for job hunters read in advance without informing them isn't really an invasion of their privacy because they are only supposed to be informed by work-related mails from our office.

12. Your lengthy supervisory experience specifically in road construction - - - - - - - - your application strong, and you were on the list of final four.

(A) enables
(B) makes
(C) certified
(D) looked

中譯 (B) 特別是在您在公路建設的長時間監管經驗，讓您的申請資格脫穎而出，而你也在最後的四人名單中。

解析 本題考題屬於『使役動詞 (make)』的考法。空格後面雖然有受詞 (application) 來接受動作，但是沒有執行被驅使動作的對象，反而是接形容詞 (strong); 所以判斷動詞應該用「使役動詞」。所以選擇答案 (B)。選項 (A) 是一般動詞用法，後面需接受詞，且受詞之後的動詞形式必須用不定詞 (to VR)，文法明顯與上下文不符，所以不選。選項 (C) 是一般動詞用法，與上下文句意不符，所以不選。(D) 是「連綴動詞」，後面需直接用接形容詞，文法明顯與上下文不符，所以不選。

超語感練習 Track 042

Your lengthy supervisory experience specifically in road construction makes your application strong, and you were on the list of final four.

13. In Japan, firms don't - - - - - - - - reluctant to recruit staff to uncomplainingly endure much longer work weeks than they can in western countries like the US or France.

(A) make
(B) get
(C) seem
(D) see

中譯 (C) 在日本，比起能在西方國家，如美國和法國招募到的員工而言，企業相當樂意招聘毫無怨言、且能忍受更長工時的員工。

解析 本題考題屬於『連綴動詞 (seem)』的考法。空格後面直接用形容詞，所以判斷動詞應該用「連綴動詞」，所以選擇選 (C)。選項 (A)、(B) 是「使役動詞」，要有受詞，與文法不符，所以不選。選項 (D) 是一般動詞用法時，要有受詞，與文法不符，所以不選。

超語感練習 Track 043

In Japan, firms don't seem reluctant to recruit staff to uncomplainingly endure much longer work weeks than they can in western countries like the US or France.

14. In an important memorandum to staff, the CEO pointed out that those qualified for the position should - - - - - - - - clients attached to the trading floor longer for more profits.

(A) appoint
(B) hear
(C) feel
(D) leave

中譯 (D) 在給員工的一個重要的備忘錄中，公司執行長指出，那些勝任這一職位的人，應該讓客戶待在販售商品的樓層更長的時間，以取得更多的利潤。

解析 本題考題屬於『使役動詞(leave)』的考法。空格後面雖然有執行被驅使動作的對象，但是沒有受詞所驅策的動作，反而是接形容詞(attached)；所以判斷動詞應該用選項中的「使役動詞」，故選擇答案(D)。選項(A)是一般動詞用法，後面需接受詞，文法明顯與上下文不符，所以不選。選項(B)是及物動詞用法中的「感官動詞」，因為與句意不符，所以不選。(C)是「連綴動詞」，後面需直接用接形容詞，文法明顯與上下文不符，所以不選。

超語感練習 🎧 Track 044

In an important memorandum to staff, the CEO pointed out that those qualified for the position should leave clients attached to the trading floor longer for more profits.

15. The job fair was made slightly spoilt by the complaints of one of the firm managers whose speech after the match, - - - - - - - - negative to the justice of the referee.

(A) made
(B) seemed
(C) tasted
(D) left

中譯 (B) 這場招聘會稍嫌美中不足，某位公司經理公開發表不滿言論，並質疑面試官的公正性，這部分是本次招聘會稍嫌不足的地方。

解析 本題考題屬於『連綴動詞 (seem)』的考法。空格後面直接用形容詞，所以判斷動詞應該用選項中「連綴動詞」，所以選擇選 (B)。選項 (A) 是「使役動詞」，要有執行被驅使動作的對象，與文法不符，所以不選。選項 (C) 是「連綴動詞」，與上下文句意不符，所以不選。選項 (D) 是一般動詞用法時，要有受詞，與文法不符，所以不選。

超語感練習 🎧 Track 045

The job fair was made slightly spoilt by the complaints of one of the firm managers whose speech after the match, seemed negative to the justice of the referee.

16. Well, if you and your seniors can't reach consensus on how to invite more talents to improve the fault rate, and then we will have to have the case - - - - - - - - for the arbitration sometime next week.

(A) sending
(B) send
(C) sent
(D) to send

中譯 (C) 那麼，如果你和你的長官無法針對如何招攬更多的優秀人才，進而改善故障率的事宜上達成共識，那麼，我們就必須在下個禮拜的某個時候，將案件送交仲裁。

解析 本題考題屬於『使役動詞 (have)』的考法。選項 (C) 中文解釋為「被送出的」，所以選擇答案 (C)。選項 (A) 是現在分詞 (V-ing) 用法，表示主動行為，句意明顯與上下文不符，所以不選。選項 (B) 是動詞原形用法，但因為沒有驅使的動作的對象，不可能接動詞原形，所以不選。選項 (D) 是不定詞，與文法不符，所以不選。

超語感練習 Track 046

Well, if you and your seniors can't reach consensus on how to invite more talents to reduce the fault rate, and then we will have to have the case sent for the arbitration sometime next week.

17. Ms. Fleming chose the company because she felt that it -------- her salary offered compatible with her talents and experience.

(A) made
(B) helped
(C) tasted
(D) felt

中譯 (A) Fleming 小姐選擇這間公司，因為她覺得這間公司提供了一個與她的天分和經驗相等值的薪水。

解析 本題考題屬於『使役動詞 (make)』的考法。空格後面有受詞 (salary)，所以先排除「連綴動詞」的用法，所以先剔除選項 (C)、(D)。而「使役動詞」後面需接動詞 (VR) 或形容詞來補充說明受詞的狀態。因為受詞之後沒有可以驅使的對象，所以不可能接動詞，只能接形容詞。選項 (B) 使役動詞 (helps) 後面可以接靜態、動態形容詞；因為句意明顯與上下文不符，所以不選。選項 (A) 使役動詞 (makes) 因為句意與上下文相符，所以這題選擇答案 (A)。

超語感練習 🎧 Track 047

Ms. Fleming chose the company because she felt that it made her salary offered compatible with her talents and experience.

18. I am aware that you have many years of experience in this field, which has the board - - - - - - - - that you have the qualification to hold a management position.

(A) to be convinced
(B) convince
(C) convincing
(D) convinced

中譯 (B) 我知道你在這個領域有多年經驗，而這讓董事會確信，你有資格掌有這個管理職位。

解析 本題考題屬於『使役動詞 (have)』的考法。使役動詞中，have 後面接動詞 (VR) 或形容詞來補充說明受詞的狀態，而且受詞後面有接受動作的對象（that 名詞子句），所以用動詞原形。

超語感練習  Track 048

I am aware that you have many years of experience in this field, which has the board convince that you have the qualification to hold a management position.

19. If supervisors first deal with what bothers or worries employees about their work in the job seeking fair, the supervisors will have the booths - - - - - - - - for maximum performance and efficiency.

(A) be established
(B) establish
(C) established
(D) establishing

中譯 (C) 如果上級能先處理員工在就業博覽會的崗位上，所遭遇的煩惱或憂慮的話，這將讓這些架設在展場的攤位有最高的性能和效率。

解析 本題考題屬於『使役動詞 (have)』的考法。後面的結構雖然有驅使的對象，但是因為沒有驅使對象的動詞，所以只能接選項中的『動態形容詞』用法中被動意涵的過去分詞，所以選擇答案 (C)。答案 (A) 出現 be 動詞，與上下文的文法不符，所以不選。答案 (B) 是動詞用法與上下文的文法不符，所以不選。答案 (D) 是動詞的現在用法，意味著主動、進行，句意明顯與上下文不符，所以不選。

超語感練習 Track 049

If supervisors first deal with what bothers or worries employees about their work in the job seeking fair, the supervisors will have the booths established for maximum performance and efficiency.

20. The board was satisfied to find the successful candidate - - - - - - - - good initiative, judgment, and adaptability as well as a willingness to subordinate his own ambition for the good of a team.

(A) to display
(B) displayed
(C) display
(D) displaying

中譯　(D) 董事會滿意地發現，一個成功的候選人應當會顯示出良好的主動性、判斷力和應變能力，以及願意為了團體的利益去馴服他自己的野心。

解析　本題考題屬於『認為 (find)』的考法。『認為』動詞中，上下文的句意中，既是指雇主希望求職者所展現的特質，是為主動行為，所以應當用現在分詞 (V-ing) 用法，所以答案選 (D)。選項 (A) 是不定詞用法，與文法不符，所以不選。選項 (B) 是動詞過去式或過去分詞，與文法不符，所以不選。選項 (C) 是動詞原形用法，且在一個句子中沒有做適當的變化，與文法不符，所以不選。

超語感練習　 Track 050

The board was satisfied to find the successful candidate displaying good initiative, judgment and adaptability as well as a willingness to subordinate his own ambition for the good of a team.

21. All applicants for the position will be considered - - - - - - - -
for this opening.
   (A) equal
   (B) equally
   (C) to equal
   (D) equaled

中譯　**(B)** 所有此職缺的申請人，將會在這個職位空缺中給予相等程度地考
　　　 慮。

解析　considered「考慮的」，是形容詞，以副詞修飾形容詞，故選為副詞詞
　　　 性的 (B) 選項。選項 (A) 為形容詞、選項 (C) 為不定詞、選項 (D) 為過去
　　　 式動詞。

超語感練習　🎧 Track 051

All applicants for the position will be considered
equally for this opening.

22. Despite initial resistance from middle management, the
- - - - - - - - to focus on product placement is now being taken
seriously by the board of directors.
(A) suggest
(B) suggested
(C) suggesting
(D) suggestion

中譯 (D) 儘管原本來自中階主管的反抗，但專注在產品佈置的建議現在已經
被執行長董事會認真看待。

解析 the 是定冠詞，用在名詞前，故選擇名詞 (D)。選項 (A) 為動詞、選項
(B) 為過去式動詞、選項 (C) 為 Ving。

超語感練習 Track 052

Despite initial resistance from middle management,
the suggestion to focus on product placement is now
being taken seriously by the board of directors.

23. It might seem like an oversimplification, but it is the mutual communication skills that - - - - - - - Mark's interview distinguished.

(A) make
(B) build
(C) feel
(D) seem

中譯　(A) 這樣講似乎是過於簡單化，但正是相互的溝通技巧突顯出 Mark 的面試表現。

解析　本題考題屬於『使役動詞(make)』的考法。空格後面雖然有執行被驅使動作的對象，但是沒有受詞所驅策的動作，反而是接形容詞 (distinguished)；所以判斷動詞應該用「使役動詞」。所以選擇答案 (A)。選項 (B) 是一般動詞用法，句意明顯與上下文不符，所以不選。選項 (C)、(D) 是「連綴動詞」，後面需接形容詞，與文法不符，所以不選。

超語感練習　🎧 Track 053

It might seem like an oversimplification, but it is the mutual communication skills that make Mark's interview distinguished.

24. Employees we want to invite are in a need of working in areas where they have to expose themselves to hazardous substances, and have them - - - - - - - - appropriate protective clothing for others to exchange.

(A) issued
(B) issue
(C) issuing
(D) to issue

中譯 (B) 我們希望招募的員工，是需要讓自己暴露於危險物質地點工作的人，並讓他們發放適當的防護衣給其他人，以供替換。

解析 本題考題屬於『使役動詞 (have)』的考法。使役動詞中，have 後面的受詞需接動詞 (VR) 或形容詞來補充說明受詞的狀態，而且受詞後面有接受動作的對象 (clothing)，所以用動詞原形，所以答案選 (B)。

超語感練習 Track 054

Employees we want to invite are in a need of working in areas where they have to expose themselves to hazardous substances, and have them issue appropriate protective clothing for others to exchange.

25. The aim of our course is to help you - - - - - - - - the anxiety that most people have when speaking in front of many interviewers.

(A) overcoming
(B) to be overcome
(C) overcame
(D) overcome

中譯 (D) 本課程的目的是幫助你克服大多數人都有的焦慮，那就是在很多面試官面前講話。

解析 本題考題屬於『使役動詞 (help)』的考法。使役動詞中，help 後面的受詞需接動詞 (VR)、不定詞 (to VR) 或形容詞來補充說明受詞的狀態，而且受詞後面有接受動作的對象 (anxiety)，所以用動詞原形，所以答案選 (D)。

超語感練習 🎧 Track 055

The aim of our course is to help you overcome the anxiety that most people have when speaking in front of many interviewers.

26. In cooperation with Management Training Consultants Inc., our company will have newcomers - - - - - - - - the new professional development program that will begin in the spring.

(A) take
(B) taken
(C) took
(D) to take

Unit 1 Unit 2 Unit 3 Unit 4 Unit 5 Unit 6 Unit 7 Unit 8 Unit 9 Unit 10

中譯 (A) 在與「管理培訓顧問」合作之下，我們的公司會讓新人參加將在春天展開的新的職業發展計劃。

解析 本題考題屬於『使役動詞 (have)』的考法。使役動詞中，have 後面的受詞需接動詞 (VR) 或形容詞來補充說明受詞的狀態，而且受詞後面有接受動作的對象 (development program)，所以用動詞原形，所以答案選 (A)。

超語感練習 🎧 Track 056

In cooperation with Management Training Consultants Inc., our company will have newcomers take the new professional development program that will begin in the spring.

27. The town re-elected the mayor by a - - - - - - - - of more than 10% over his nearest rival.

(A) margin
(B) amount
(C) quantity
(D) measure

中譯　(A) 鄉長重選，與得票數最接近的對手差幅超過百分之十。

解析　此題為單字題型，依照題意，應該選擇 (A) 選項 margin「差數」。其餘選項中文解釋分別為 (B) 數量、(C) 品質及 (D) 尺寸。

 超語感練習　Track 057

The town re-elected the mayor by a margin of more than 10% over his nearest rival.

28. One reason that lawyers earn such large sums of money is the ever - - - - - - - - size of the damages awarded in civil courts.

(A) increased
(B) increasing
(C) increasingly
(D) increase

中譯　(B) 律師賺得如此多金額的原因之一，是因為民事法庭增加傷害賠償金額程度。

解析　size 為名詞，應該以形容詞修飾名詞，但在 4 個選項當中，並沒有形容詞，故選擇以現在分詞當形容詞，來修飾名詞 size「大小程度」，此題選 (B)。而其他選項詞性分別為 (A) 過去式動詞、(C) 副詞、(D) 動詞。

超語感練習 🎧 Track 058

One reason that lawyers earn such large sums of money is the ever increasing size of the damages awarded in civil courts.

29. Although it is true that we were colleagues for a time, we worked in different departments, which made it - - - - - - - - to come into contact with each other very often.

(A) tough
(B) toughen
(C) toughly
(D) toughened

中譯 (A) 雖然我們同事一段時間這是事實，然而我們在不同的部門工作，而這使得彼此頻繁相互接觸是困難的。

解析 本題考題屬於『使役動詞 (make)』的考法。make 後面接受詞後，因為沒有驅使的對象，所以不可能接動詞，只能接『靜態形容詞』，所以選擇答案 (A)。答案 (B) 是動詞用法，句意明顯與上下文不符，所以不選。答案 (C) 是副詞用法，句意明顯與上下文不符，所以不選。答案 (D) 是動詞的過去式或過去分詞用法，句意明顯與上下文不符，所以不選。

超語感練習 🎧 Track 059

Although it is true that we were colleagues for a time, we worked in different departments, which made it tough to come into contact with each other very often.

30. If supervisors first deal with what bothers or worries employees about their work in the job seeking fair, the supervisors will have the booths - - - - - - - - for maximum performance and efficiency.

(A) be established
(B) establish
(C) established
(D) establishing

中譯 (C) 如果上級能先處理員工在就業博覽會的崗位上，所遭遇的煩惱或憂慮的話，這將讓這些架設在展場的攤位有最高的性能和效率。

解析 本題考題屬於『使役動詞 (have)』的考法。後面的結構雖然有驅使的對象，但是因為沒有驅使對象的動詞，所以只能接選項中的『動態形容詞』用法中被動意涵的過去分詞，所以選擇答案 (C)。答案 (A) 出現 be 動詞，與上下文的文法不符，所以不選。答案 (B) 是動詞用法與上下文的文法不符，所以不選。答案 (D) 是動詞的現在用法，意味著主動、進行，句意明顯與上下文不符，所以不選。

超語感練習 🎧 Track 060

If supervisors first deal with what bothers or worries employees about their work in the job seeking fair, the supervisors will have the booths established for maximum performance and efficiency.

擬真試題

1. After all applications are received, the city council - - - - - - - - a meeting to choose new marketing contractors for the new outlet plaza.

   (A) held
   (B) holds
   (C) hold
   (D) will hold

中譯 (D) 在收到所有的申請文件之後，市議會將召開會議，為新的購物廣場選擇新的行銷承包商。

解析 上下文的句意中，關鍵字句為附屬子句的「現在簡單式」，暗示著「現在時間」或者「不確定的未來」；而上下文的句意適合用「未來」的動作來表示將要發生的事件，所以答案選 (D)。

超語感練習  Track 061

After all applications are received, the city council will hold a meeting to choose new marketing contractors for the new outlet plaza.

2. Concern about the future of many marine animals - - - - - - - -
to a rapid reduction in trading of marine products recently,
especially those made from international conserved ones.
(A) leads
(B) has led
(C) leading
(D) lead

中譯 (B) 最近對於許多海洋動物未來的擔憂，導致海洋產品交易迅速減少，
特別是那些來自國際保護物種的產品。

解析 上下文的句意中，關鍵字句為 recently「最近地」，表示從「以前」到
「講話時」的動作或經驗持續狀態，應該用「完成式」，所以答案選
(B)。

超語感練習 　Track 062

Concern about the future of many marine animals
has led to a rapid reduction in trading of marine
products recently, especially those made from
international conserved ones.

3. The mental reinforcements in ensuring product validity
   - - - - - - - - damage throughout the upcoming price-cutting
   competition.
   (A) minimizes
   (B) will minimize
   (C) minimized
   (D) minimize

中譯　(B) 在心理上強化保證產品的正當性，會在整個即將到來的削價競爭中
　　　將損害降到最低。

解析　上下文的句意中，upcoming「即將到來的」，表示「未來」時間，所
　　　以答案選 (B)。

超語感練習 　Track 063

The mental reinforcements in ensuring product
validity will minimize damage throughout the
upcoming price-cutting competition.

4. Although the output situation seems poor at the moment, we - - - - - - - - a swift improvement once the downturn is over.

(A) anticipated
(B) anticipate
(C) will anticipate
(D) are anticipate

中譯 (C) 雖然輸出的情況目前看來不佳，但衰退一旦結束，我們預計會迅速改善。

解析 上下文的句意中，關鍵字句為 once，表示「預計」狀態，屬「未來」時間的用法，所以答案選 (C)。

超語感練習 Track 064

Although the output situation seems poor at the moment, we will anticipate a swift improvement once the downturn is over.

5. I -------- to inform you that the expired date of your insurance in this product warranty will be further extended as of June 15th for one more year via our promotion campaign.

(A) write
(B) will write
(C) writing
(D) am writing

中譯 (D) 這封信是為了告訴你，透過我們產品的促銷，您這個產品保固的保險到期日將進一步於 6 月 15 日起被延長一年。

解析 本題為 TOEIC 書信體中慣用的書信告知／通知開頭寫法。用意是，讓讀這封信或訊息的人，在讀時如同告知者正在跟被告知者敘述一件事的原委，所以用「現在時間進行式」。所以答案選 (D)。

超語感練習 🎧 Track 065

I am writing to inform you that the expired date of your insurance in this product warranty will be further extended as of June 15th for one more year via our promotion campaign.

6. We ------- several interesting variations on the original business model to you, which we have experienced for a long time.

(A) presented
(B) are presenting
(C) have presented
(D) will be present

中譯 (B) 我們將呈現給你一些、針對原有商業模式的有趣變化，而這已經實驗了一段時間。

解析 關鍵字句為 have experienced，表示「現在時間完成式」，意指「現在當下」的狀態；而上下文的句意中，「現在時間進行式」指當下行為，所以答案選 (B)。

 超語感練習 Track 066

We are presenting several interesting variations on the original business model to you, which we have experienced for a long time.

7. The president's speech at tomorrow's meeting - - - - - - - -
consumers' concerns about cutbacks and downsizing of
product supplies.

(A) be addressed
(B) addressed
(C) have addressed
(D) will address

中譯 (D) 總裁在明天的會議上，將針對消費者對裁員和縮減產品供應的擔憂
發表演講。

解析 上下文的句意中，關鍵字句為 tomorrow，表示「未來」，所以整句應
當用「未來」時間的動詞形式；句意中無需用到「完成式」概念，所以
答案選 (D)。

超語感練習 🎧 Track 067

The president's speech at tomorrow's meeting will
address consumers' concerns about cutbacks and
downsizing of product supplies.

8. Ms. Decker's membership of marketing daily necessities in this region will be reissued as soon as she - - - - - - - the outstanding balance and fees.

(A) has paid
(B) will pay
(C) paid
(D) pays

中譯　(D) 當 Decker 女士把餘額及費用給繳清時，她在這區域行銷日常用品的會員資格將重新被發給。

解析　上下文的句意中，關鍵字句為 as soon as，表示「只要……就……」；附屬子句用「現在簡單式」來代替「未來簡單式」，所以答案選 (D)。

超語感練習　Track 068

Ms. Decker's membership of marketing daily necessities in this region will be reissued as soon as she pays the outstanding balance and fees.

9. Despite the size of your order and our current business volume, we are confident we ----- - - - - the production deadline.

(A) living up to
(B) will live up to
(C) live up to
(D) lived up to

中譯 (B) 儘管因為您的訂單與我們目前業務量的大小，我們有信心將達成生產的最後期限。

解析 關鍵字句為 are，表示「現在時間簡單式」；附屬子句上下文句意應當用「未來簡單式」，所以答案選 (B)。

超語感練習 🎧 Track 069

Despite the size of your order and our current business volume, we are confident we will live up to the production deadline.

10. The annual market representative seminar is - - - - - - - - on Monday January 15th in the cafeteria from 9 a.m. until noon.

(A) about to hold
(B) to be held
(C) going to hold
(D) about to holding

中譯 (B) 每年的市場代表人員研討會，將於1月15日，從上午9點到中午，在餐廳舉辦。

解析 關鍵字句為 is，表示「現在時間」；而上下文句意應當表示「即將發生的事件」，且為被動用法，所以用 beV + VR 表示「未來事件」，所以答案選 (B)。

超語感練習 🎧 Track 070

The annual market representative seminar is to be held on Monday January 15th in the cafeteria from 9 a.m. until noon.

11. A demolition crew - - - - - - - - clearing the bad debts property in the marketing section even before the proper permits were issued by the headquarters.

(A) will begin
(B) is beginning
(C) had begun
(D) has begun

中譯　(C) 甚至在總部發出適當的許可證之前，拆遷人員已經開始清理行銷部門的壞賬資產。

解析　上下文的句意中，關鍵字句為 even before，表示「從……開始」，且在附屬子句中是屬於後發生的行為；所以早發生是用「完成式」的基本概念，所以答案選 (C)。

超語感練習　Track 071

A demolition crew had begun clearing the bad debts property in the marketing section even before the proper permits were issued by the headquarters.

12. The delay could not have been prevented because the local agents failed to achieve monthly quota until two weeks later than we - - - - - - - -.
(A) are anticipated
(B) have anticipated
(C) are anticipating
(D) had anticipated

 中譯 (D) 延遲無法避免，因為當地的代理商比我們預期的晚兩個星期達成每月配額。

解析 上下文的句意中，關鍵字句為 later than，表示「比……晚……」，且主要子句為「過去時間簡單式」；附屬子句中的動作為晚發生的事件，用「過去時間完成式」以表示事件先後，所以答案選 (D)。

 **超語感練習** Track 072

The delay could not have been prevented because the local agents failed to achieve monthly quota until two weeks later than we had anticipated.

13. Originally, we all thought the organization - - - - - - - the duty to the famous marketing agency before the news was announced, but it was later proven to be a false step.

(A) attributed
(B) has attributed
(C) attributes
(D) is attributing

中譯 **(B)** 本來，在消息公佈之前，大家都以為這間機構已委任知名的市場行銷公司，但後來被證明是錯誤的一步。

解析 關鍵字句為過去時間的動詞形式 (thought, annunced, was proven)；上下文的句意中表示原先預想更早的狀況，所以用「過去時間完成式」以表示事件先後，所以答案選 (B)。

超語感練習 🎧 Track 073

Originally, we all thought the organization has attributed the duty to the famous marketing agency before the news was announced, but it was later proven to be a false step.

14. In the past ten years, according to the statistics, the number of Americans using 90 percent of their disposable income to purchase redundant goods instead of paying off credit card debts - - - - - - - - by 30 percent.

(A) has been rising
(B) will have risen
(C) was rising
(D) has risen

中譯 (D) 據統計，在過去的十年中，美國人會使用90％的可支配收入購買多餘的物品，而不是去還清信用卡欠款的數量，這樣的人就成長了三成。

解析 關鍵字句為過去時間(the past ten years)；上下文的句意中，強調當下「從過去已經持續一段時間的狀態或行為」，所以用「現在時間完成式」，所以答案選(D)。

超語感練習 🎧 Track 074

In the past ten years, according to the statistics, the number of Americans using 90 percent of their disposable income to purchase redundant goods instead of paying off credit card debts has risen by 30 percent.

15. Anyone nominated for a position on the fair committee responsible for making marketing policies - - - - - - - - to fill out a background information sheet designed to help the board evaluate their qualifications.

(A) will have been needed
(B) have been needed
(C) will be needed
(D) will need

中譯　(D) 任何被提名為博覽會委員會此一職位、負責制定營銷政策的人，將需填寫背景資料，以幫助董事會評估其資格。

解析　上下文的句意中，前因後果判斷理當接主動的未來的動作狀態，所以用「未來時間簡單式」，所以答案選 (D)。

超語感練習　🎧 Track 075

Anyone nominated for a position on the fair committee responsible for making marketing policies will need to fill out a background information sheet designed to help the board evaluate their qualifications.

16. The extremely poor sales figures we witnessed over the recent summer months - - - - - - - - a dramatic effect on the supply industry, which is essentially crucial in revenue.

(A) are having
(B) have been
(C) have had
(D) has had

中譯 (D) 我們看到，最近夏季月份的銷售數字十分不佳，這對供應業產生相當的影響，而供應業在營收中扮演十分重要的角色。

解析 關鍵字句為 over the recent summer months，表示「從過去到現在的一段時間」。所以用「現在時間完成式」，所以答案選 (D)。

超語感練習 Track 076

The extremely poor sales figures we witnessed over the recent summer months have had a dramatic effect on the supply industry, which is essentially crucial in revenue.

17. Marketing information indicates that pesticide companies
- - - - - - - testing procedures to determine the levels at
which toxic substances were harmful to humans to innovate
the products concerned.

(A) develop
(B) developing
(C) had developed
(D) had been developed

中譯 (C) 行銷資料上說明著，殺蟲劑公司已經展開測試程序，以確定有毒物質對人體的有害程度，進而改革相關產品。

解析 關鍵字句為 were；因為從上下文的句意中，「開發」此一事實較早發生，所以應用早發生的「完成式」。又遇到過去時間，所以用「過去時間完成式」，所以答案選 (C)。

超語感練習 🎧 Track 077

Marketing information indicates that pesticide companies had developed testing procedures to determine the levels at which toxic substances were harmful to humans to innovate the products concerned.

18. As of this coming Tuesday, Allen Potter - - - - - - - - the head of Research and Development in marketing for five years.
   (A) to be
   (B) was
   (C) had been
   (D) will have been

中譯　(D) 從這個星期二起，Allen Potter 將以身為研究和開發的營銷負責人此一身份滿五年。

解析　關鍵字句為 coming（即將到來的），表示未來的狀態。又有時間點 (for five years) 表示「一段時間」，所以用「未來時間完成式」，所以答案選 (D)。

超語感練習　🎧 Track 078

As of this coming Tuesday, Allen Potter will have been the head of Research and Development in marketing for five years.

19. The newspaper's chief editor, who is well-known for his demanding expectations, rarely - - - - - - - deadlines for his journalists as well as the least sales number of each issue.

(A) extending
(B) extended
(C) extend
(D) extends

中譯　(D) 這家報紙的主編對人期待甚高，眾所周知，他很少為他的記者延長期限，與增加每期的最低銷售數量。

解析　這個句子沒有特殊的關鍵字句或時間、動作先後。所以句子中表現出一般現在事實，所以答案選 (D)。

超語感練習　🎧 Track 079

The newspaper's chief editor, who is well-known for his demanding expectations, rarely extends deadlines for his journalists as well as the least sales number of each issue.

20. The promotion items we strongly recommended
-------- everything we needed for our campaign, from
accommodations and transport to meals and event tickets
with satisfying discounts.
(A) will provide
(B) provided
(C) provide
(D) has provided

中譯 (B) 我們強烈推薦的促銷項目中，提供我們宣傳所需要的一切，從住
宿、交通到膳食，甚至是包準滿意的折扣的門票。

解析 這個句子沒有特殊的關鍵字句或時間、動作先後。所以句子中表現出一
般過去事實，所以答案選 (B)。

超語感練習  Track 080

The promotion items we strongly recommended
provided everything we needed for our campaign,
from accommodations and transport to meals and
event tickets with satisfying discounts.

21. - - - - - - - - analysis of last year's sales will not be available until the end of March.

(A) Complete
(B) Completely
(C) To complete
(D) Completing

中譯 **(A)** 去年銷售報表完整的分析，將不會在三月底前取得。

解析 選項 (B) 為完成地（副詞）；選項 (C) 為完成（不定詞）；選項 (B) 為完成（動詞＋ing）。在名詞 analysis「分析」前以形容詞 complete「完成的」修飾，complete analysis「完成的分析」是名詞片語，故選 A。

超語感練習 🎧 Track 081

Complete analysis of last year's sales will not be available until the end of March.

聽新多益 Part 5，第一次就拿閱讀高分

22. After months of disagreement and having sold all his remaining stock, the chairman resigned from the board of
--------.

(A) supervisors
(B) anchors
(C) directors
(D) administrators

中譯　(C) 在連續幾個月都持不同意見，及賣掉所有他剩下的股票之後，主席請辭執行長董事一職。

解析　此題為單純的單字考題，選項 (A) 為監督人；選項 (B) 為錨；選項 (C) 為執行長；選項 (D) 為行政官員，依題意選擇選項 (C) 執行長。

超語感練習　🎧 Track 082

After months of disagreement and having sold all his remaining stock, the chairman resigned from the board of directors.

23. The response to the new advertising was - - - - - - - - negative that the company was forced to rethink its whole marketing philosophy.

(A) so
(B) very
(C) much
(D) too

超語感練習　🎧 Track 083

The response to the new advertising was so negative that the company was forced to rethink its whole marketing philosophy.

24. Tablet computers - - - - - - - - very popular over the past couple of years, and they are expected to continue to outsell all other types of computers for the foreseeable future.

(A) become

(B) have become

(C) are becoming

(D) had become

中譯 (B) 平板電腦在這幾年已變得十分受歡迎，我們在可預見的未來仍預期其銷量上將勝過其他種類的電腦。

解析 本句的時間為 over the past couple of years「這幾年來」，表示敘述這幾年來已發生的事，所以應該用現在完成式 (has/have + pp)，而 become 的三態為 become–became–become，故選 B。選項 (A) 為現在式、選項 (C) 為現在進行式、選項 (D) 則為過去完成式，此 3 選項皆與題意不符。

超語感練習  Track 084

Tablet computers have become very popular over the past couple of years, and they are expected to continue to outsell all other types of computers for the foreseeable future.

25. The introduction of the new sales technique had a - - - - - - - -
effect on the company's market share.
(A) notice
(B) noticing
(C) noticed
(D) noticeable

中譯　(D) 新引進的銷售技巧在公司的市佔率上有顯著的影響。

解析　"effect"「影響」，是名詞，需以形容詞修飾名詞，故選 (D) 顯著的。選項 (A) 為動詞、選項 (B) 為現在分詞、選項 (C) 為過去分詞。

超語感練習　🎧 Track 085

The introduction of the new sales technique had a
noticeable effect on the company's market share.

　聽新多益 Part 5，第一次就拿閱讀高分

26. There is growing - - - - - - - - for the need for online marketing within the fashion industry.

(A) accept
(B) accepting
(C) acceptance
(D) accepted

中譯 (C) 時尚界裡的網路行銷接受度正在增長中。

解析 "growing"「增長中的」，是形容詞，以形容詞修飾名詞，故選 (C) 接受。選項 (A) 為動詞、選項 (B) 為動名詞、選項 (D) 為形容詞。

超語感練習 Track 086

There is growing acceptance for the need for online marketing within the fashion industry.

27. Your reservation for three nights at the Royal Plaza Hotel
- - - - - - - - all meals is confirmed.

(A) include
(B) included
(C) including
(D) inclusive

中譯 (C) 你在 Royal Plaza 飯店的訂位包含所有餐點已確認。

解析 副詞子句的主詞與主要子句主詞相同時，可將副詞子句中的連接詞與主詞改成現在分詞，即為分詞構句。including = which includes ，關係代名詞 which，代表 Your reservation「你的訂位」。

 超語感練習 Track 087

Your reservation for three nights at the Royal Plaza Hotel including all meals is confirmed.

28. Star Fashion is an institution that is famous in many countries for - - - - - - - - use of bright colors and patterns.
(A) their
(B) them
(C) they
(D) its

中譯　(D) 星流行是一個機構，因為它的亮色系和圖樣，在許多國家都享富盛名。

解析　"its"「它的」，代表 "Star Fashion"「星流行」。在 4 個選項中，僅有 (A) 和 (D) 為所有格，(A) 為「他們的」(D) 為「它的」(單數)，故選 (D)。而選項 (B) 為「他們」的受格，而選項 (C) 為主格。

超語感練習　Track 088

Star Fashion is an institution that is famous in many countries for its use of bright colors and patterns.

29. Small businesses often - - - - - - - - a much more personalized service than their larger competitors.
(A) offered
(B) offer
(C) offering
(D) offers

中譯 (B) 小商家們常常比他們較大的競爭對手，提供較為個人化的服務。

解析 頻率副詞 often「常常」，表示事情是常態的，所以是現在式，選擇現在式動詞，故選 (B)。選項 (D) 亦為現在式動詞，但是有加第三人稱單數 s，主詞是複數的 Small businesses「小商家們」，所以不能選 (D)。

超語感練習 Track 089

Small businesses often offer a much more personalized service than their larger competitors.

30. Withdrawal from the trade agreement was - - - - - - - but finally rejected.

(A) consider
(B) considering
(C) considered
(D) to consider

中譯 (C) 退出貿易協議被列入考慮，但是最後仍被駁回。

解析 過去式被動語態，主詞＋ was/were ＋過去分詞，故選 (C)。例句：People trafficking was noticed by our government.（人口販運的這一個問題被我們的政府注意到。）

超語感練習 🎧 Track 090

Withdrawal from the trade agreement was considered but finally rejected.

擬真試題

1. A sheer variety of products that we offer for sale are
- - - - - - - - unmatched by any of our competitors.

(A) distinctive
(B) distinctively
(C) distinct
(D) distinctness

中譯 (B) 我們的銷售產品多元，對我們的任何競爭對手而言，非常明顯地是
無法比擬。

解析 空格之後是動詞所變化而來的形容詞用法，而空格之前為 beV; 該空格
由本句句意中知道用以強化形容詞 (unmatched)，所以該詞性應該用
「副詞」。

超語感練習 Track 091

A sheer variety of products that we offer for sale are
distinctively unmatched by any of our competitors.

2. All production is halted, and until the company's profits get improved by 5%, neither side seems - - - - - - - - to negotiate.
(A) preparation
(B) preparing
(C) prepare
(D) prepared

中譯 (D) 所有的生產停止，且在公司利潤提升至5%前，雙方似乎還未能準備好進行協商。

解析 空格之前為「連綴動詞」，連綴動詞之後應該用形容詞，而且本句句意中沒有用到修飾句子、動詞或其他結構的用法，所以答案選 (D)。此句主詞為人或者是擬人化的對象，動詞 prepare 應當用過去分詞 (V-p.p.) 形式，來表達人或者是擬人化的對象接受動作。

超語感練習  Track 092

All production is halted, and until the company's profits get improved by 5%, neither side seems prepared to negotiate.

3. Foreign businessmen often express - - - - - - - - amazement at how far our manufacturer can achieve what they originally think impossible.

(A) unexpecting
(B) unexpect
(C) unexpected
(D) unexpective

中譯 (C) 外國商人對於我們的製造廠商的表現驚訝，因為製造廠商達成了他們原本認為不可能的事情。

解析 空格之前為一般動詞，空格之後為名詞；按照本句句意，應當屬形容詞為前位修飾，就進修飾之後的名詞。動詞 unpexpected 當形容詞用時，應當用過去分詞 (V-p.p.) 形式表達被動語態，所以答案選 (C)。

超語感練習 🎧 Track 093

Foreign businessmen often express unexpected amazement at how far our manufacturer can achieve what they originally think impossible.

4. In spite of consumer objection, Infocus will spend - - - - - - - -
time expanding the potential benefits of building cell phone
plants.

(A) consider

(B) considerate

(C) considerable

(D) consideration

中譯 (C) 儘管消費者的反對，Infocus 還是會花費相當長的時間，擴大建設
手機工廠的潛在好處。

解析 空格之前為一般動詞，空格之後為名詞；所以，按照本句句意，空格應
當為修飾不可數名詞的前位修飾語、表示「相當的」的中文意思，所以
答案選 (C)。

 超語感練習 **Track 094**

In spite of consumer objection, Infocus will spend
considerable time expanding the potential benefits of
building cell phone plants.

5. Stunned by the - - - - - - - - performance of the production yield these years, the magazine critic was at a loss for words when he sat down to write a review of the firm.

(A) impress
(B) impressed
(C) impressively
(D) impressive

中譯　(D) 當雜誌評論家坐下來寫這間公司的評論時，對其這些年令人印象深刻的生產良率訝異到說不出話來。

解析　空格之後為不可數名詞；修飾不可數名詞的前位修飾語應當用形容詞，所以答案選 (D)。選項 (B) 是動詞的 V-p.p. 所衍生而來的形容詞用法，暗指所修飾對象的「被動、完成」狀態，與上下文不符，所以不選。

超語感練習　🎧 Track 095

Stunned by the impressive performance of the production yield these years, the magazine critic was at a loss for words when he sat down to write a review of the firm.

6. Setting up plants in the commercial districts brings - - - - - - - - more profits than in the industrial ones because there is always more consumption in the former ones.

(A) more
(B) even
(C) so
(D) too

（中譯） **(B)** 在商業區設廠，比在工業區帶來了更多的多的利潤，因為在前者的消費量總是較多。

（解析） 空格之前為一般動詞，空格之後為形容詞＋名詞的結構；所以，按照本句句意，空格應當為強化形容詞的副詞前位修飾語、表示「更……的」的中文意思，所以答案選 (B)。

超語感練習　Track 096

Setting up plants in the commercial districts brings

even more profits than in the industrial ones because

there is always more consumption in the former

ones.

7. Construction contractors with high adaptability in their products are - - - - - - - - to apply for the positions on assembly lines because of the extensive mobile demands.
(A) eligibility
(B) eligibleness
(C) eligible
(D) eligibly

中譯 (C) 因為大量的機動性要求配合度高的承包商有資格去申請在組裝線上的職缺。

解析 空格之前為 beV，beV 之後應該用形容詞，而且本句句意中沒有用到修飾句子、動詞或其他結構的用法，所以答案選 (C)。

超語感練習 Track 097

Construction contractors with high adaptability in their products are eligible to apply for the positions on assembly lines because of the extensive mobile demands.

8. After a heated debate, the factory director and assistant manager in production department both returned to their - - - - - - - - offices.

(A) respective
(B) respectful
(C) respectable
(D) respected

中譯 (A) 經過激烈的辯論，廠長和生產部門的副經理均回到了各自的辦公室。

解析 空格之前為限定詞中的所以格用法，空格之前為名詞，而修飾名詞應當用「形容詞」來當名詞的「前位修飾語」，而且本句句意中沒有用到修飾句子、動詞或其他結構的用法，所以答案選 (A)。選項 (B) respectful，英英解釋為 "feeling or showing respect"，解釋為「尊重人的，表示敬意的，有禮貌的」，與上下文不符，所以不選。選項 (C) respectable，英英解釋為 "be approved of by society and considered to be morally correct"，解釋為 "值得尊重的，人格高尚的"，與上下文不符，所以不選。選項 (D) respected，中文解釋為「受尊敬的」，與上下文不符，所以不選。

 超語感練習 Track 098

After a heated debate, the factory director and assistant manager in production department both returned to their respective offices.

9. It was incredibly - - - - - - - - of the director to give the assembly employees the extra bonus for the overtime.

(A) considerable
(B) considerate
(C) consider
(D) consideration

中譯 **(B)** 老闆為加班的裝配線員工加額外的獎金,真是體貼到令人難以相信。

解析 空格之前為副詞,副詞應該當形容詞的前位修飾語,用來修飾之後的形容詞;所以答案選 (B):「體貼的」。選項 (A) 中文翻譯為「相當多的;相當大的」。

超語感練習 🎧 Track 099

It was incredibly considerate of the director to give the assembly employees the extra bonus for the overtime.

10. Mr. Thomson is a good leader for the reason that he is able to provide - - - - - - - - criticism in a way that most people are receptive to.

(A) constructs
(B) constructor
(C) constructive
(D) construction

中譯 (C) 湯姆森先生是一個很好的領導者，因為他能提供大多數人都樂於接受的建設性批評。

解析 空格之後為名詞，修飾名詞應該用形容詞，所以答案選 (C)。

超語感練習 🎧 Track 100

Mr. Thomson is a good leader for the reason that he is able to provide constructive criticism in a way that most people are receptive to.

11. The company has threatened to lay off all 400 manufacturing workers if production doesn't resume - - - - - - - -, but labor leaders have said that they will ignore such 'crude threats' and continue to work towards a mutually acceptable solution to the situation.

(A) short
(B) shortly
(C) shortingly
(D) shorted

中譯 (B) 該公司曾威脅，如果不趕緊恢復生產，要裁員 400 個製造業工人，但工會領導人表示，他們會忽略這樣的「粗魯的威脅」，並繼續朝著雙方都能接受的解決方案來努力。

解析 空格之前為一般動詞，一般動詞之後應當接副詞做後位修飾語來修飾動詞。選項 (C) 並無此單字用法，所以答案選 (B)。

超語感練習 🎧 Track 101

The company has threatened to lay off all 400 manufacturing workers if production doesn't resume shortly, but labor leaders have said that they will ignore such 'crude threats' and continue to work towards a mutually acceptable solution to the situation.

12. In preparation for the quarterly inner audit, many directors are bidding for the completion of a - - - - - - - - screening system in the complex.

(A) permanent
(B) permanently
(C) permanence
(D) permeate

中譯　(A) 在準備每季內部審計工作時，很多主管努力投標，好讓永久的檢視系統得以於複合型住商大樓裡建設完成。

解析　空格之前為限定詞的不定冠詞用法，空格之後為修飾對象名詞 (system)。所以用形容詞當做前位修飾語來修飾名詞，所以答案選 (A)。選項 (D) 為動詞用法，與上下文法不符，所以不選。

超語感練習  Track 102

In preparation for the quarterly inner audit, many directors are bidding for the completion of a permanent screening system in the complex.

13. All of the employees have been quite - - - - - - - - with the auditor during the routine career safety examination of the company.

(A) cooperate

(B) cooperative

(C) cooperating

(D) cooperation

中譯　(B) 公司在進行例行的職業安全檢查時,所有的員工一直以來都相當配合審計師。

解析　空格之前為修飾形容詞的副詞用法,空格之後為與形容詞相搭配的介系詞。從上下文的句意中知道,空格應選用形容詞,所以答案選 (B)。

超語感練習　Track 103

All of the employees have been quite cooperative

with the auditor during the routine career safety

examination of the company.

14. Distribution service of merchandise will be launched as
-------- as possible after the warehouse outage problem
has been resolved.

(A) quick
(B) quickly
(C) quicken
(D) quickness

中譯 (B) 在倉庫的停電問題解決之後，商品的配送將儘速啟動。

解析 as… as 的原級比較中，可以接副詞或形容詞，其中修飾動詞，所以用「副詞」用法。

超語感練習 Track 104

Distribution service of merchandise will be launched
as quickly as possible after the warehouse outage
problem has been resolved.

15. Consumer perspectives are becoming an - - - - - - - - critical factor in determining the way merchandise is presented and packaged.

(A) increase
(B) increased
(C) increasing
(D) increasingly

中譯 (D) 在決定商品呈現及包裝的方式上，消費者的觀點正變成為越來越重要的因素。

解析 空格之前為限定詞的不定冠詞用法，空格之後為形容詞。從上下文的句意中知道，空格應選用副詞來修飾形容詞，所以答案選 (D)。

超語感練習 🎧 Track 105

Consumer perspectives are becoming an increasingly critical factor in determining the way merchandise is presented and packaged.

16. The Cosmetics Division has publicly refused to produce any facial cream which claims to provide - - - - - - - - unbelievable rejuvenation results and skin altering benefits.

(A) an amount of
(B) a deal of
(C) a number of
(D) a sum of

中譯 (C) 化妝品部門已公開拒絕生產任何號稱有許多驚人回春成果和改變膚質的面霜。

解析 空格之後為修飾名詞的「前位修飾語」，中文翻成「許多」。而且後面名詞為可數用法 (results)，所以答案選 (C)。其他選項都是修飾不可數名詞，所以不選。

超語感練習  Track 106

The Cosmetics Division has publicly refused to produce any facial cream which claims to provide a number of unbelievable rejuvenation results and skin altering benefits.

17. The frost damage in the fruit is - - - - - - - - of an even more severe agricultural problem that should be immediately addressed as far as the balance between supply and demand is concerned.

(A) indicate
(B) indicated
(C) indication
(D) indicative

中譯 (D) 就供給與需求之間的平衡而言，水果的凍害表明了是個更嚴重的農業問題，且應立即處理。

解析 空格之前為 beV，beV 之後出現形容詞相搭配用法的介系詞，從上下文的句意中知道，空格應選用形容詞，所以答案選 (D)。

超語感練習 🎧 Track 107

The frost damage in the fruit is indicative of an even more severe agricultural problem that should be immediately addressed as far as the balance between supply and demand is concerned.

18. Usually as quiet as a mouse in the office, Peter showed a much - - - - - - - - aspect to his aggressive personality while debating for the quality perfection with other production line employees.

(A) bolder
(B) bold
(C) boldest
(D) boldly

中譯　(A) Peter 平時在辦公室安靜得像隻老鼠，但與其他生產線員工為品質完美而辯論時，他卻大膽地展現出他人格激進的一面。

解析　空格之前為副詞 (much)，空格之後出現名詞，所以空格應該選「形容詞」。從上下文的句意中知道，much 此一副詞用來強化形容詞，中文翻成「更……的多……」，所以答案選 (A)。

超語感練習  Track 108

Usually as quiet as a mouse in the office, Peter showed a much bolder aspect to his aggressive personality while debating for the quality perfection with other production line employees.

19. Many customers are changing their car insurance to The Great Tree because its promoting campaign is by far the most - - - - - - - -.

(A) persuasion
(B) persuasively
(C) persuade
(D) persuasive

中譯 (D) 許多客戶正在將他們的汽車保險改到 The Great Tree 公司，因為它的推廣活動是目前為止最有說服力的。

解析 空格之前為副詞 (most)，副詞之後可以是副詞或形容詞放句尾；而強化副詞或形容詞最高級用 by far the ＋最高級，所以空格應該選「形容詞」，所以答案選 (D)。

超語感練習 🎧 **Track 109**

Many customers are changing their car insurance to The Great Tree because its promoting campaign is by far the most persuasive.

20. On account that his reckless response to the questions, which was less than - - - - - - - -, the yield rate panel decided to deny his acceptance into their quality control program.
(A) satisfaction
(B) satisfied
(C) satisfactory
(D) satisfying

中譯 (C) 由於他回答這些問題很輕率，使得答覆不盡如人意，良率專案組決定拒絕接受他成為品質控管計畫的一員。

解析 空格之前為 beV(was)，且 beV 之後出現副詞 (less) 修飾形容詞，從上下文的句意中知道，空格應選用形容詞，所以答案選 (C)。其他選項由動詞主、被動所衍生出的形容詞用法，與上下文句意不符，所以不選。

超語感練習 🎧 Track 110

On account that his reckless response to the questions, which was less than satisfactory, the yield rate panel decided to deny his acceptance into their quality control program.

21. The National Health Agency advised pharmaceutical companies that all herbal remedies travelers brought from China - - - - - - - - in the same way as western drugs.

(A) have been licensed

(B) be licensed

(C) should license

(D) licensed

中譯　(B) 國民健康局呼籲製藥公司，觀光客從中國帶進的所有草藥療法要如同西藥一樣，被發給執照許可。

解析　本題考題屬於『意志動詞』的考法。由句中連接詞(that)與動詞(advised)判斷，空格的動詞應當用「助動詞(should)」加上「動詞原形(VR)」；又由上下句意判斷，應該要用「被動」，所以答案選(B)。

超語感練習 　Track 111

The National Health Agency advised pharmaceutical companies that all herbal remedies that travelers brought from China be licensed in the same way as western drugs.

22. Injuries and illnesses - - - - - - - - reduced by a road construction program if it had been strictly followed and had enforcement appropriate to civilians' interests.

(A) could have been
(B) could have
(C) could be
(D) have been

 (A) 若道路施工計畫有嚴格遵守，並依民眾利益適當執行，那麼因其而造成的傷害與疾病就會減少。

解析 本題考題屬於『假設語氣』考法中，與「過去時間」相反的假設。由句中連接詞 (if) 與動詞 (had been… followed) 判斷，空格的動詞應當用與「過去時間」相反的「過去完成式」；但是因為是「主要子句」，需要「過去式助動詞 (could) ＋完成式 (have V-p.p.)」，又由上下句意判斷，應該要用「被動」，所以答案選 (A)。

超語感練習 🎧 Track 112

Injuries and illnesses could have been reduced by a road construction program if it had been strictly followed and had enforcement appropriate to civilians' interests.

23. The problems with the just-in-time supply chain were solved
following - - - - - - - - with the lead suppliers.
(A) demands
(B) arguments
(C) negotiations
(D) concessions

中譯 (C) 與即時供應連鎖商的問題被解決,接著與重要的供應商協商。

解析 此題為單字題,選項 (A) 為請求;選項 (B) 為爭論;選項 (D) 為讓步,用
法為+ to/from。依照題意,應選擇選項 (C) 協商最為恰當。

超語感練習 🎧 Track 113

The problems with the just-in-time supply chain were
solved following negotiation with the lead suppliers.

24. Reliability is the cornerstone of Cabot Engineering's success, and so it is the responsibility of all employees to guarantee - - - - - - - -.

(A) it

(B) them

(C) its

(D) that

中譯　(A) 可靠性是 Cabot 工程的成功基石，所以保證它的可靠性是全體員工的責任。

解析　代名詞 it「它」，表示主詞 reliability「可靠性」，故選 (A)。

超語感練習  Track 114

Reliability is the cornerstone of Cabot Engineering's success, and so it is the responsibility of all employees to guarantee it.

25. The man talking on the radio about the lack of - - - - - - - -
after the accident at the oil refinery is getting increasingly
angry.

(A) payment
(B) refunds
(C) remittance
(D) compensation

中譯 (D) 在廣播上談論有關於在油品精煉廠發生意外之後賠償金不足的男
人，愈講愈生氣。

解析 此題為單字題，依照題意，應該選擇選項(A) 賠償金最為恰當。其他選
項單字中文解釋則分別為(A) 報償、(B) 退費、及(C) 匯款。

超語感練習 Track 115

The man talking on the radio about the lack of
compensation after the accident at the oil refinery is
getting increasingly angry.

26. After the accident, all electrical - - - - - - - must be checked before any further use.
(A) facilities
(B) hardware
(C) assets
(D) equipment

中譯 **(D)** 意外事件之後，所有用電的設備必須在進一步使用之前檢查。

解析 此題為單字題，依照題意，應該選擇選項 (D) 設備最為恰當。其他選項單字中文解釋則分別為 (A) 設施、(B) 硬體、及 (C) 資產。

超語感練習 Track 116

After the accident, all electrical equipment must be checked before any further use.

27. Sales of Mongolia-made products climb - - - - - - - - from $500 million in 2012 to more than $600 million last year.

(A) progressed
(B) progressing
(C) progressive
(D) progressively

中譯　(D) 蒙古製造的產品銷售逐步攀升，從 2012 年的 5 億美元，到去年超過 6 億美元。

解析　空格之前為一般動詞，一般動詞之後應該用副詞加以強化動詞的動作，所以答案選 (D)。

超語感練習　🎧 Track 117

Sales of Mongolia-made products climb progressively from $500 million in 2012 to more than $600 million last year.

28. There is so much competition in products that prices are
- - - - - - - - likely to stay low.
(A) height
(B) highlily
(C) high
(D) highly

中譯 **(D)** 產品上如此多的競爭，讓價格很有可能會停留在低點。

解析 空格之前為 beV，beV 之後已經出現形容詞 (likely)；所以，修飾形容詞
應當用副詞用法，所以答案選 (D)。選項 (A) 是名詞，中文翻譯為「高
度」，與上下文不符，所以不選。選項 (B) 無此用法。選項 (C) 是形容
詞，中文翻譯為「高的」，與上下文不符，所以不選。

超語感練習 Track 118

There is so much competition in products that prices
are highly likely to stay low.

29. When considering two fabric samples for a new product, Mr. Sox always picks up the - - - - - - - of the two.
(A) cheaply
(B) cheaper
(C) cheapest
(D) cheap

中譯　(B) Sox 先生為了新產品在兩種織物樣品間做考量時,總是拿起兩個之中較便宜的那個。

解析　後面出現特定字句 (of the two),表示是考比較級中「兩者其中一個的⋯⋯」比較級用法,所以答案選 (B)。選項 (A) 為副詞,與上下文法不符,所以不選。選項 (C) 為形容詞最高級用法,與上下文法不符,所以不選。選項 (D) 為形容詞原級,與上下文法不符,所以不選。

超語感練習　　Track 119

When considering two fabric samples for a new product, Mr. Sox always picks up the cheaper of the two.

30. The franchise rendered by the merchant should be sent
- - - - - - - - the end of this month, or we might forfeit the
opportunity.
(A) less than
(B) no better than
(C) no sooner than
(D) no later than

中譯 (D) 由商家提供的專營權最晚應該會於本月底送達，否則我們可能喪失
這個機會。

解析 空格之前為動詞(sent)，且空格之後出現時間副詞(the end of this
month)，從上下文的句意中知道，空格應選用修飾時間副詞的副詞用
法，且上下文句意要的是「不晚於……」的中文，所以答案選(D)。

超語感練習 Track 120

The franchise rendered by the merchant should be
sent no later than the end of this month, or we might
forfeit the opportunity.

擬 真 試 題

1. Delegating easier - - - - - - - - projects to inexperienced workers while leaving challenging ones with veterans is suggesting the office operate more efficiently.

    (A) purchased
    (B) purchasing
    (C) purchase
    (D) be purchased

中譯 (B) 委派容易採購項目給沒有經驗的工人，然而留給那些具有挑戰性的項目給老手，是希望（建議）辦公室能更有效地運作。

解析 本題屬於『動名詞』的考法。由上下文句意判斷，while 所前後連接的部分，兩句的主詞 (delegating 與 leaving) 與後面的受詞所判斷，空格應當是「動名詞 (V-ing) ＋ N」的結構，意味著是「既定之事實」；所以，後面結構應搭配「動名詞 (V-ing)」，以符合上下文句意，所以答案選 (B)。

超語感練習 Track 121

Delegating easier purchasing projects to inexperienced workers while leaving challenging ones with veterans is suggesting the office operate more efficiently.

2. All shipment and packaging waste is under the request of -------- of, and collected in the agreed receptacles near the rear entrance of the building.

(A) being disposed
(B) to dispose
(C) disposing
(D) dispose

中譯　(A) 依要求，所有廢棄物的裝運應集中在集收地做處理。該集收地靠近大樓後方入口處，是經同意而選出的地方。

解析　本題屬於『動名詞』的考法。空格因為前有「介系詞」的關係，只能接「動名詞」。由上下文句意判斷，應當用「被動語態」。所以答案選 (A)。

超語感練習  Track 122

All shipment and packaging waste is under the request of being disposed of, and collected in the agreed receptacles near the rear entrance of the building.

3. We understand that you are arranging for immediate delivery from stock, and we look forward to - - - - - - - - from you soon.

(A) hear
(B) hearing
(C) be hearing
(D) to be heard

中譯 (B) 我們了解您正在從存貨中安排現貨，以便立即發貨，而我們也期待著能從您那裡儘快得到消息。

解析 本題屬於『動名詞』的考法。上下文關鍵字是 look forward to 的介系詞 to，後面結構應當用「動名詞 (V-ing)」；且為「主動」用法，所以答案選 (B)。

超語感練習 🎧 Track 123

We understand that you are arranging for immediate delivery from stock, and we look forward to hearing from you soon.

4. The controversial law regarding team share buying restrictions continues - - - - - - - - across the country by various local community retailers.

(A) to have protested
(B) to protest
(C) to be protesting
(D) to be protested

中譯　(D) 關於球隊股份購買限制的法律引起極大的爭議，抗議聲浪不斷，遍及全國各零售單。

解析　本題屬於『不定詞』的考法。上下文關鍵字是 continue，後面結構應當用「不定詞 (to VR)」。由上下文句意判斷，應當用「被動語態」，所以答案選 (D)。

超語感練習 Track 124

The controversial law regarding team share buying restrictions continues to be protested across the country by various local community retailers.

5. With so much shipment company information on the Internet, it is difficult to urge users - - - - - - - - your website, place orders, and even confirm delivery orders precisely.

(A) to be noticing
(B) to notice
(C) noticing
(D) noticed

中譯 (B) 由於網路到處都是貨運公司的資訊，因此很難督促使用者留意你的網站、下訂單，甚至確認訂貨訂單。

解析 本題屬於『不定詞』的考法。上下文關鍵字是 urge，後面結構應當用「不定詞 (to VR)」。由上下文句意判斷，應當用「主動語態」，所以答案選 (B)。

超語感練習 🎧 Track 125

With so much shipment company information on the Internet, it is difficult to urge users to notice your website, place orders, and even confirm delivery orders precisely.

6. An outsider cannot but - - - - - - - - to understand the complexity of the development concerning the automated transportation process as it has evolved today.

(A) struggles
(B) struggled
(C) to struggle
(D) struggle

中譯 (D) 局外人不得不努力去理解自動運輸過程演變至今的複雜發展。

解析 本題屬於『不定詞』的考法。上下文關鍵字是 cannot but，後面結構應當用「不定詞 (to VR)」，其中 to 是省略的。所以答案選 (D)。

超語感練習  Track 126

An outsider cannot but struggle to understand the complexity of the development concerning the automated transportation process as it has evolved today.

7. Some customers prefer - - - - - - - - a minimum order they placed each month to pouring in large amounts for delivery discounts.

(A) to maintain
(B) is maintaining
(C) maintained
(D) maintaining

中譯 (D) 有些客戶喜歡保持他們每個月所訂購的最低數量，更勝於浥注大量數量所得來的折扣。

解析 本題屬於『動名詞』的考法。上下文關鍵字是 prefer… to…，因為 to 後面結構是「動名詞(V-ing)」，所以 prefer 後面的動詞形式也應該用 V-ing，以達到同特質的物件、比較目的，所以答案選 (D)。

超語感練習 🎧 Track 127

Some customers prefer maintaining a minimum order they placed each month to pouring in large amounts for delivery discounts.

8. The purchase meeting is likely - - - - - - - - at headquarters soon, but we will notify participants when an official location has been set.

(A) to take the place
(B) to taking place
(C) take place
(D) to take place

中譯 (D) 採購大會可能很快在總部舉行，但當正式的場地決定時，我們會通知與會人員。

解析 本題屬於『不定詞』的考法。上下文關鍵字是 likely，選用「發生、舉辦」的片語為「take place」，為「主動」用法，後面結構應當用「不定詞 (to VR)」，所以答案選 (D)。

超語感練習 🎧 Track 128

The purchase meeting is likely to take place at headquarters soon, but we will notify participants when an official location has been set.

9. Road transportation tends ------- comparatively cheaper and more direct than rail, and in the past few years, haulage has doubled in the UK.

(A) to becoming
(B) to become
(C) to became
(D) to be become

中譯 (B) 公路運輸趨向於變得相對地比較便宜，並且比鐵路更直接，而且，在過去的幾年中，貨運業在英國已成長一倍。

解析 本題屬於『不定詞』的考法。關鍵字是 tend（意欲……），由上下文句意判斷，後面結構應當用「不定詞 (to VR)」，所以答案選 (B)。

超語感練習 Track 129

Road transportation tends to become comparatively cheaper and more direct than rail, and in the past few years, haulage has doubled in the UK.

10. In order - - - - - - - - others in net proceeds, crews responsible for purchasing orders must have good communication skills with those in Logistics Department.

(A) to be outnumbered
(B) to outnumber
(C) to have outnumbered
(D) to outnumbering

中譯 **(B)** 為了在淨收益的數量上勝過其他人,負責採購部門人員都必須擁有與物流部門人員良好溝通的能力。

解析 本題屬於『不定詞』的考法。由上下文句意判斷,選用「為了要」的中文,應當用「不定詞(to VR)」表示「目的、企圖性」,所以答案選 (B)。

超語感練習 Track 130

In order to outnumber others in net proceeds, crews responsible for purchasing orders must have good communication skills with those in Logistics Department.

11. The rapid growth of express delivery service makes us anticipate - - - - - - - - efficiency in prompt delivery that becomes more indispensable part of the quarterly profit and loss account.

(A) to continuing
(B) continuing
(C) to continue
(D) continue

中譯 (B) 由於快遞業務成長快速，我們開始期待能持續達成有效率的快遞服務，並讓快遞服務的效率成為季損益帳中不可或缺的一部分。

解析 本題屬於『動名詞』的考法。上下文關鍵字是 anticipate，後面結構應當用「動名詞 (V-ing)」，所以答案選 (B)。

超語感練習 Track 131

The rapid growth of express delivery service makes us anticipate continuing efficiency in prompt delivery that becomes more indispensable part of the quarterly profit and loss account.

12. It is not sophisticated for the company - - - - - - - - solely on one import source to meet the demand for parts production, instead of searching for possible cooperation with other sources.

(A) to rely
(B) to relying
(C) to be relied
(D) to be relying

中譯 (A) 公司僅僅依靠一個進口來源來滿足零件生產的需求，而不是尋找其它可能的來源進行合作的這件事，並不複雜。

解析 本題屬於『不定詞』的考法。由上下文句意判斷，選用「為了要……」的中文，且有「虛主詞 (it)」出現，應當用「不定詞 (to VR)」，所以答案選 (A)。

超語感練習 Track 132

It is not sophisticated for the company to rely solely on one import source to meet the demand for parts production, instead of searching for possible cooperation with other sources.

13. On accepting your order, we will enclose a debit note for this purchase amount, and shall appreciate - - - - - - - your credit note by return, and in the hope to be deposited directly into our savings accounts specified by the salespeople by the end of this month.

(A) receiving
(B) to receive
(C) to be receiving
(D) to received

中譯 **(A)** 一收到您的訂單後，我們將會附上一張購買金額的借條，感激收到您的信用票據回應，並希望您於本月前直接匯入我們銷售人員所指定的儲蓄賬戶。

解析 本題屬於『動名詞』的考法。上下文關鍵字是 appreciate，後面結構應當用「動名詞 (V-ing)」，所以答案選 (A)。

超語感練習 🎧 Track 133

On accepting your order, we will enclose a debit note for this purchase amount, and shall appreciate receiving your credit note by return, and in the hope to be deposited directly into our savings accounts specified by the salespeople by the end of this month.

14. Many importers and exporters, however, prefer - - - - - - - - their costs by dealing with clearing or forwarding agents in the countries of their supplies to cutting down on expenses by laying off employees.

(A) to reduce
(B) reducing
(C) reduce
(D) be reduced

中譯 (B) 然而，許多進口商和出口商，寧願以處理清算或轉介其供應國家代理商的方式，來削減開支，而不願用裁員方式降低開支。

解析 本題屬於『動名詞』的考法。上下文關鍵字是 prefer，後面結構應當用「動名詞 (V-ing)」，所以答案選 (B)。prefer 後面如果有比較的對象時，以比較對象的連接詞或介系詞為動詞變化依據。後面結構有 to + V-ing (to cutting down…)，所以答案選 (B)。

超語感練習 Track 134

Many importers and exporters, however, prefer reducing their costs by dealing with clearing or forwarding agents in the countries of their supplies to cutting down on expenses by laying off employees.

15. The manager has encouraged Mr. Brade - - - - - - - - for the position abroad responsible for mutual orders as well as trust matters, on account of his impressive language skills in the price negotiation.

(A) have applied
(B) have been applied
(C) to apply
(D) be applied

中譯 (C) 考慮到在價格談判上、令人印象深刻的語言技能，該經理鼓勵 Brade 先生申請國外的職位，而此職位專職雙方訂單與信任的事務。

解析 本題屬於『不定詞』的考法。上下文關鍵字是 encourage，後面結構應當用「不定詞 (to VR)」。所以答案選 (C)。

超語感練習 Track 135

The manager has encouraged Mr. Brade to apply for the position abroad responsible for mutual orders as well as trust matters, on account of his impressive language skills in the price negotiation.

16. These simplified services are particularly valuable in foreign trades because of the complicated arrangements which have - - - - - - - - in advance.

(A) to making
(B) to be making
(C) to make
(D) to be made

中譯 (D) 這些簡化的服務在國外交易中尤為可貴，因為複雜的安排必須提前受理進行。

解析 本題屬於『不定詞』的考法。由上下文句意判斷，選用「不定詞 (to VR)」，又上下文句意應用「被動」，中文翻譯為「為了要被制訂……」，所以答案選 (D)。

超語感練習 Track 136

These simplified services are particularly valuable in foreign trades because of the complicated arrangements which have to be made in advance.

17. The purpose of the conference is to fix and maintain freight rates at a profitable level, and to ensure that a sufficient minimum of cargo is always forthcoming - - - - - - - - the regular sailings they undertake to provide.

(A) to be feeding
(B) to be fed
(C) to feed
(D) to feeding

中譯　(C) 本次會議的目的，是將運價確定並維持在盈利水平上，並確保總是有足夠的最小貨物量，以滿足他們所承諾提供的定期班次。

解析　本題屬於『不定詞』的考法。由上下文句意判斷，選用「不定詞 (to VR)」，且為「主動」，所以答案選 (C)。

超語感練習　🎧 Track 137

The purpose of the conference is to fix and maintain freight rates at a profitable level, and to ensure that a sufficient minimum of cargo is always forthcoming to feed the regular sailings they undertake to provide.

18. Mechanical handling permits - - - - - - - - of cargoes in a matter of hours rather than days, thus reducing the time ships spend in port, and greatly increasing the number of sailings.

(A) to loaded
(B) loading
(C) to be loaded
(D) to be loading

中譯　(B) 機械裝卸的方式以允許貨物裝載在幾個小時內完成，而不需耗時幾天；如此一來，可以減少船舶在港口花費的時間，而大大地增加班次的數量。

解析　本題屬於『動名詞』的考法。上下文關鍵字是 permit，後面結構因為沒有受詞，應當用「動名詞 (V-ing)」，所以答案選 (B)。

超語感練習  Track 138

Mechanical handling permits loading of cargoes in a matter of hours rather than days, thus reducing the time ships spend in port, and greatly increasing the number of sailings.

19. Merchants should make it a routine - - - - - - - - the strengths of each shipping company in order to use their potentials to full advantage.

(A) to assess
(B) for assessing
(C) assess
(D) assessed

中譯 (A) 商家應該讓評估各個船公司的長處一事，成為例行公事，以便充分利用其潛力。

解析 本題屬於『不定詞』的考法。由上下文句意判斷，選用「為了要」的中文，且有「虛主詞(it)」出現，應當用「不定詞(to VR)」，所以答案選 (A)。

超語感練習 🎧 Track 139

Merchants should make it a routine to assess the strengths of each shipping company in order to use their potentials to full advantage.

20. You are requested not - - - - - - - - the transmission but to send it with the barcode for warranty claim processing and the information stated in the "return delivery" section to the service test centre.

(A) disassemble
(B) to disassemble
(C) disassembled
(D) to be disassembled

中譯　(B) 請您不要拆開變速器，而是將其此機器連同用於保修申請處理的條碼、和「退貨」部分中聲明的資訊，一起發送到服務檢測中心。

解析　本題屬於『不定詞』的考法中的「意志動詞」考法。由上下文關鍵字為 request；由句意判斷，動詞形式應當選用「不定詞(to VR)」的答案，所以答案選(B)。

超語感練習　🎧 Track 140

You are requested not to disassemble the transmission but to send it with the barcode for warranty claim processing and the information stated in the "return delivery" section to the service test centre.

21. The new cargo railway being constructed south of the city will be no use - - - - - - - it faster for people to commute from the suburban neighborhoods to urban ones.

(A) making
(B) make
(C) to make
(D) made

中譯　(A) 正在城市南部建設中的新貨運鐵路,將無助於讓通勤的人們,從郊區地區到城市上下班更為快速。

解析　本題屬於『動名詞』的考法。上下文關鍵字是 no use,後面結構省略掉介系詞 (in),所以應當用「動名詞 (V-ing)」,所以答案選 (A)。

超語感練習　Track 141

The new cargo railway being constructed south of the city will be no use making it faster for people to commute from the suburban neighborhoods to urban ones.

22. On account of the demanding deadline of the production delivery, Ms. Potter admit - - - - - - - - to choose the factory hiring a few more seasonal workers to ease the stress of overburdened employees.

(A) to decide
(B) to be decided
(C) to be deciding
(D) deciding

中譯 (D) 由於產品運輸的期限急迫，Potter 女士決定選擇有僱用幾個季節性工人的工廠，以減輕員工負擔過重的壓力。

解析 本題屬於『動名詞』的考法。上下文關鍵字是 admit（承認），後面結構應當用「動名詞 (V-ing)」；且為「主動」用法，所以答案選 (D)。

超語感練習 🎧 Track 142

On account of the demanding deadline of the production delivery, Ms. Potter admits deciding to choose the factory hiring a few more seasonal workers to ease the stress of overburdened employees.

23. Unfortunately the expected end-of-year orders never
- - - - - - -, leaving the company order book nearly empty.

(A) come in
(B) came in
(C) had come in
(D) has come in

中譯　(B) 不幸地，預期年底的訂單從未進來，留下幾乎空白的公司訂購帳冊。

解析　語意中，表示訂單未進來是已發生的事，故是過去式，故選 (B)。come「來」的動詞三態為 come–came–come。

超語感練習　Track 143

unfortunately the expected end-of-year orders never came in, leaving the company order book nearly empty.

24. Due to - - - - - - - - snow in southern England, many flights from Heathrow Airport have been delayed for up to seven hours.

(A) large
(B) heavy
(C) abundant
(D) oversize

中譯 (B) 由於英國南部劇烈的降雪，許多從希斯洛機場的航班延誤七小時以上。

解析 此題為單字題，依照題意，應該選擇選項 (B)heavy 劇烈的最為恰當，一般如雨及雪等的天氣情況會以 heavy 形容，例如 heavy rain, heavy snow…。其他選項單字中文解釋則分別為 (B) 大的、(C) 豐富的、及 (D) 過大的。

超語感練習 Track 144

Due to heavy snow in southern England, many flights from Heathrow Airport have been delayed for up to seven hours.

25. During the expansion of Hong Kong International Airport, some flights will be -------- to Macau.
(A) sent
(B) transported
(C) diverted
(D) relocated

中譯 **(D)** 在香港國際機場擴建期間，一些航班將會被轉移到澳門。

解析 此題為單字題，will be 後面應該加被動式動詞，4 個選項皆符合，所以依照題意，應該選擇選項 (C)diverted 轉移最為恰當。其他選項單字中文解釋則分別為 (A) 送、(B) 運輸、及 (D) 重新安置。

超語感練習 🎧 Track 145

During the expansion of Hong Kong International Airport, some flights will be diverted to Macau.

26. As we will be making regular shipments, we wondered whether you could arrange open cover - - - - - - - - £60,000 against all risks to insure consignments to North and South American Eastern seaboard ports.

(A) by
(B) in
(C) for
(D) with

中譯 (C) 由於我們即將進行定期的運輸，我們想知道，你是否能針對所有從北美和南美東海岸港口的貨物風險，安排總計 60,000 英鎊的預約保險單。

解析 本題考題屬於『介系詞』考法中「介系詞＋名詞」的考法。從上下文句意判斷，介系詞的中文翻譯為「總計……」，所以答案選 (C)。

超語感練習 Track 146

As we will be making regular shipments, we wondered whether you could arrange open cover for £60,000 against all risks to insure consignments to North and South American Eastern seaboard ports.

27. Details - - - - - - - - regard to packing and values are attached, and we would be grateful if you could quote a rate covering all risks from port to port.

(A) in
(B) at
(C) on
(D) with

中譯 (D) 一併附上關於包裝和價值方面的細節，如果你能針對港口與港口間的所有風險加以報價，我們將不勝感激。

解析 本題考題屬於『介系詞』考法中「介系詞＋名詞」的考法。從上下文句意判斷，是為片語「關於……(with regard to)」的中文，所以答案選(D)。

超語感練習 🎧 Track 147

Details with regard to packing and values are attached, and we would be grateful if you could quote a rate covering all risks from port to port.

28. We called - - - - - - - - the order which was placed with you by telephone this morning for the following details.

(A) to confirm
(B) confirm
(C) confirming
(D) to confirming

中譯 **(A)** 我們打電話來向您確認，您今天上午透過電話所下訂單的細節。

解析 本題屬於『不定詞』的考法。由上下文句意判斷，需要代表「企圖、目的」的句意，所以用「不定詞 (to VR)」，答案選 (A)。

超語感練習 Track 148

We called to confirm the order which was placed with you by telephone this morning for the following details.

29. Please forward these purchase documents to your correspondent in Munich, which are worth - - - - - - - - them with deliberation to the consignee against acceptance of our 60 days draft.

(A) to hand
(B) to be handed
(C) handing
(D) to be handing

中譯　(C) 請把這些採購文件，轉寄給在慕尼黑的聯絡人員，這些文件值得審慎交付給反對接受我們 60 天匯票的收件人。

解析　本題屬於『動名詞』的考法。上下文關鍵字是 worth，後面結構應當用「動名詞 (V-ing)」，所以答案選 (C)。

超語感練習 　Track 149

Please forward these purchase documents to your correspondent in Munich, which are worth handing them with deliberation to the consignee against acceptance of our 60 days draft.

30. I have enclosed a copy of their receipt from their goods depot at Köln, and you can have any other documents that we can supply - - - - - - - - you with your claim.

(A) to help
(B) to helping
(C) to be helped
(D) to helped

中譯 (A) 我隨信附上，來自他們在 Köln 倉庫的貨物收據複印本，而且你可以有，因應您的要求、我們所幫忙提供的其他文件。

解析 本題屬於『不定詞』的考法。由上下文句意判斷，由上下文句意判斷，主詞是人，應當用主動，且用帶有「企圖、目的」句意的「不定詞 (to VR)」，所以答案選 (A)。

超語感練習 Track 150

I have enclosed a copy of their receipt from their goods depot at Köln, and you can have any other documents that we can supply to help you with your claim.

擬真試題

1. Could you please send me details of the refrigerators - - - - - - - - in yesterday's 'Evening Post'?

   (A) advertising
   (B) advertised
   (C) advertise
   (D) advertises

中譯 (B) 請你能不能寄給我昨天在 "晚間郵報" 廣告的冰箱細節？

解析 本題屬於『過去分詞』的考法。由上下文結構判斷，空格雖然為「動詞」選項，但是因為與前句並沒有「連接詞」存在，推測應當是省略「連接詞(which/that)」，所以選擇「動詞(are advertised)」變成「分詞(advertised)」的答案；且動詞與名詞的關係應該為「被動」用法，是為「被廣告」的對象，所以答案選 (B)。

超語感練習 Track 151

Could you please send me details of the refrigerators advertised in yesterday's 'Evening Post'?

2. Visitors in the stadium are quite - - - - - - - - by our Model Info 2, the newest solar battery.

(A) impressed
(B) impressing
(C) impress
(D) impresses

中譯　(A) 展場的參訪者對我們的最新的太陽能電池－信息 2 號機型印象深刻。

解析　本題屬於『情緒動詞』中『過去分詞』的考法。用「過去分詞」修飾人的情緒，是因為人的情緒由外在因素所「被動誘發」，中文翻成「使人感到……」，用以修飾講話者被影響的情緒，所以答案選 (A)。

超語感練習  Track 152

Visitors in the stadium are quite impressed by our Model Info 2, the newest solar battery.

3. Purchasers would find details of our terms in the price list
- - - - - - - - on the inside front cover of the catalogue.

(A) print
(B) printing
(C) printed
(D) prints

中譯　(C) 買家會在產品目錄封面內頁的價格表上，找到我們所印的產品規範。

解析　本題屬於『過去分詞』的考法。由上下文結構判斷，空格雖然為「動詞」選項，但是因為與前句並沒有「連接詞」存在，推測應當是省略「連接詞(which/that)」，所以選擇「動詞(is printed)」變成「分詞(printed)」的答案；且動詞與名詞的關係應該為「被動」用法，是為「被列印」的對象，所以答案選 (C)。

超語感練習　Track 153

Purchasers would find details of our terms in the
price list printed on the inside front cover of the
catalogue.

4. If you would like demonstrations of any models in the catalogue, we would be happy to arrange for our representatives - - - - - - - - on you whenever convenient.
(A) call
(B) called
(C) calling
(D) calls

中譯 (C) 如果您想看在目錄中的任何模組的演示，我們將樂意為您安排我們的代表，在您方便的時候拜訪您。

解析 本題屬於『現在分詞』的考法。由上下文結構判斷，空格雖然為「動詞」選項，但是因為與前句並沒有「連接詞」存在，推測應當是省略「連接詞 (who)」，所以選擇「動詞 (calls)」變成「分詞 (calling)」的答案；且動詞與名詞的關係應該為「主動」用法，所以答案選 (C)。

超語感練習 Track 154

If you would like demonstrations of any models in the catalogue, we would be happy to arrange for our representatives calling on you whenever convenient.

5. We highly recommend this book with - - - - - - - - description of mysterious creatures in ancient fables, and with insight into the possible origins of them.

(A) detail

(B) detailed

(C) details

(D) detailing

中譯 (B) 我們強烈推薦這本書，裡面詳細介紹遠古神話中的神秘生物、並以精闢的見解剖析他們的可能來源。

解析 本題屬於『過去分詞』的考法。由上下文結構判斷，空格雖然為「動詞」選項，但是因為用來修飾後面「名詞 (description)」，所以「動詞 (detail)」變成「分詞 (detailed)」答案，中文翻譯為「被詳細敘述的……」；且動詞與名詞的關係應該為「被動」用法，所以答案選 (B)。

超語感練習 Track 155

We highly recommend this book with detailed description of mysterious creatures in ancient fables, and with insight into the possible origins of them.

6. Our - - - - - - - online stationery shop is committed to providing students and business people with a wide variety of high-quality stationery items as well as PC products and other services.

(A) newly-established
(B) newly-establishing
(C) newly-establish
(D) new-established

中譯 (A) 我們新成立的網路文具店致力為學生和商務人士服務，提供各種高品質的文具、電腦產品與其他服務。

解析 本題屬於『複合形容詞』的綜合考法。由上下文句意判斷，動詞 (establish) 與名詞的關係應當是被動，又搭配副詞加以修飾動詞，所以答案選 (A)。

超語感練習 Track 156

Our newly-established online stationery shop is committed to providing students and business people with a wide variety of high-quality stationery items as well as PC products and other services.

7. When - - - - - - - - to customers' enquiries, be sure you have answered every query in the exhibition.

(A) replies
(B) reply
(C) replying
(D) replied

中譯 (C) 在回答客戶的詢問時，請確保您已經回答了展場的每個詢問。

解析 本題屬於『分詞構句』中的『現在分詞』考法。由上下文結構判斷，空格雖然為「動詞」選項，且有「連接詞 (when)」存在，但是因為沒有「主詞」，所以「動詞 (reply)」變成「分詞 (replying)」答案；且動詞與主詞的關係應該為「主動」用法，所以答案選 (C)。

超語感練習 🎧 Track 157

When replying to customers' enquiries, be sure you

have answered every query in the exhibition.

8. Your request will take effect in two days, and we will arrange a technical representative to instruct your employees for operation as - - - - - - - - upon purchase.
(A) guarantee
(B) is guarantee
(C) guarantees
(D) guaranteed

中譯 (D) 正如您的購買所保證的，你的要求將在兩天後生效，而且我們會安排技術代表人員去指導您的員工進行操作。

解析 本題屬於『過去分詞』的考法。由上下文結構判斷，空格雖然為「動詞」選項，但是因為與前句並沒有「主詞」存在，推測應當是省略「主詞(which/that)」，所以選擇「動詞(is guaranteed)」變成「分詞(guaranteed)」的答案；且動詞與名詞的關係應該為「被動」用法，所以答案選(D)。

超語感練習  Track 158

Your request will take effect in two days, and we will arrange a technical representative to instruct your employees for operation as guaranteed upon purchase.

9. We today display separately a range of models and samples specially - - - - - - - for their hard-wearing qualities under any critical circumstances.

(A) selected
(B) select
(C) selecting
(D) selects

中譯 (A) 我們今天個別展示一系列的模組和樣本，這組特選系列耐磨，能抵擋任何嚴峻的情況。

解析 本題屬於『過去分詞』的考法。由上下文結構判斷，空格雖然為「動詞」選項，但是因為與前句並沒有「連接詞」存在，推測應當是省略「連接詞(which/that)」，所以選擇「動詞(is selected)」變成「分詞(selected)」的答案；且動詞與名詞的關係應該為「被動」用法，所以答案選(A)。

超語感練習 🎧 Track 159

We today display separately a range of models and samples specially selected for their hard-wearing qualities under any critical circumstances.

10. In the case of a soft-binding, your documents are applied to the front and back cover, which has a distinctive marble design effect, - - - - - - - a neat and attractive finish.
(A) produce
(B) produced
(C) producing
(D) produces

中譯 (C) 以膠裝軟皮的方式裝訂，您的內文會放在特殊大理石紋的封面和封底裡，整體呈現俐落、迷人的風格。

解析 本題屬於『分詞構句』中的『現在分詞』考法。由上下文結構判斷，空格雖然為「動詞」選項，但是因為沒有「連接詞」，推測應當是省略「連接詞(which/that)」，所以選擇「動詞(produces)」變成「分詞(producing)」的答案；且動詞與主詞的關係應該為「主動」用法，所以答案選(C)。

超語感練習  Track 160

In the case of a soft-binding, your documents are applied to the front and back cover, which has a distinctive marble design effect, producing a neat and attractive finish.

11. Workshops - - - - - - - - by exhibition admission staff deal with discussions including writing admission papers, preparing for the interviews and advice on completing application preparation.

(A) conducting
(B) conduct
(C) conducted
(D) conducts

中譯 (C) 研討會是由展場行政人員負責舉辦，會上討論內容包括：撰寫入學論文、準備面試，和完整的申請書準備建議。

解析 本題屬於『過去分詞』的考法。由上下文結構判斷，空格雖然為「動詞」選項，但是因為與前句並沒有「連接詞」存在，推測應當是省略「連接詞 (which/that)」，所以選擇「動詞 (is conducted)」變成「分詞 (conducted)」的答案；且動詞與名詞的關係應該為「被動」用法，所以答案選 (C)。

超語感練習 🎧 Track 161

Workshops conducted by exhibition admission staff deal with discussions including writing admission papers, preparing for the interviews and advice on completing application preparation.

12. Customers will be pleasantly surprised by the complimentary gifts - - - - - - - to any booth visitors with fabulous coupons.

(A) distributes
(B) distribute
(C) distributing
(D) distributed

中譯 (D) 消費者至各攤位時，會拿到分送給訪客的贈品和折價券，為此他們感到又驚又喜。

解析 本題屬於『過去分詞』的考法。由上下文結構判斷，空格雖然為「動詞」選項，但是因為與前句並沒有「連接詞」存在，推測應當是省略「連接詞 (which/that)」，所以選擇「動詞 (are distributed)」變成「分詞 (distributed)」的答案；且動詞與名詞的關係應該為「被動」用法，所以答案選 (D)。

 **超語感練習** Track 162

Customers will be pleasantly surprised by the complimentary gifts distributed to any booth visitors with fabulous coupons.

13. We have received a number of enquiries over keyboard parts suitable for us to offer your possible order, which seems to be a great opportunity for office renovation - - - - - - - - place this coming few months.

(A) take
(B) taken
(C) taking
(D) takes

中譯 **(C)** 我們已經收到了許多有關鍵盤零件的詢問，也正好可提供鍵盤予您下訂單購買；看來接下來幾個月會是重新翻修辦公室的好機會。

解析 本題屬於『現在分詞』的考法。由上下文結構判斷，空格雖然為「動詞」選項，但是因為與前句並沒有「連接詞」存在，推測應當是省略「連接詞(which/that)」，所以選擇「動詞(takes)」變成「分詞(taking)」的答案；且動詞與名詞的關係應該為「主動」用法，所以答案選 (C)。

超語感練習 Track 163

We have received a number of enquiries over keyboard parts suitable for us to offer your possible order, which seems to be a great opportunity for office renovation taking place this coming few months.

14. Porter's comprehensive introduction and instruction, as well as the time line of dates and events, make this book not only a reference work but also a treasure that should be purchased by any - - - - - - - - family.
(A) cultivate
(B) cultivated
(C) cultivates
(D) cultivating

中譯 (B) Porter 全面性的介紹和說明，以及日期和事件的時間線，使得這本書不僅是一個可供參考的作品，也是一個任何有文化的家庭所應購入的寶藏。

解析 本題屬於『過去分詞』的考法。由上下文結構判斷，空格雖然為「動詞」選項，但是因為用來修飾後面「名詞 (family)」，所以「動詞 (cultivate)」變成「分詞 (cultivated)」答案，中文翻譯為「被教化的……」；且動詞與名詞的關係應該為「被動」用法，所以答案選 (B)。

超語感練習 Track 164

Porter's comprehensive introduction and instruction, as well as the time line of dates and events, make this book not only a reference work but also a treasure that should be purchased by any cultivated family.

15. Taking the chance of Oversea Study Fair, I strongly recommend this university for your further study for the master's degree, for its reputation for quality is prominently - - - - - - - - in its outstanding record of academic essay publication.

(A) reflects
(B) reflect
(C) reflected
(D) reflecting

中譯 (C) 利用海外留學展這機會，我強烈推薦這所大學，為您碩士學位的進修學習，因為在其品質方面的名聲，傑出地體現在其卓越的學術文章發表記錄。

解析 本題屬於『過去分詞』的考法。由上下文結構判斷，空格為「動詞 (reflect)」選項，且動詞與名詞的關係應該為「被動」用法，所以選用「過去分詞」形式，所以答案選 (C)。

超語感練習 🎧 Track 165

Taking the chance of Oversea Study Fair, I strongly recommend this university for your further study for the master's degree, for its reputation for quality is prominently reflected in its outstanding record of academic essay publication.

16. We offer lighting to fit every need and budget, which is very affordable, available in a wide variety of colors and patterns - - - - - - - - in the expo at an immediate discount.

(A) displayed
(B) display
(C) displays
(D) displaying

中譯 (A) 我們提供照明，以適應各種需求和預算；而價錢十分實惠，且在展場中所展示的多種顏色和圖案，有立即的折扣。

解析 本題屬於『過去分詞』的考法。由上下文結構判斷，空格雖然為「動詞」選項，但是因為與前句並沒有「連接詞」存在，推測應當是省略「連接詞 (which/that)」，所以選擇「動詞 (are displayed)」變成「分詞 (displayed)」的答案；且動詞與名詞的關係應該為「被動」用法，所以答案選 (A)。

超語感練習 🎧 Track 166

We offer lighting to fit every need and budget, which is very affordable, available in a wide variety of colors and patterns displayed in the expo at an immediate discount.

17. Every month, our magazine features a comparison of new cooking products available on the market; today, we are showing five of the - - - - - - - - brands of stainless steel cookware sets to our visitors on the last day of fair here.

(A) top-sell
(B) top-sold
(C) top-selling
(D) toply-selling

中譯 (C) 每個月，我們雜誌的特色在於，比較市場上新的烹飪產品；今天，我們展示五個最暢銷品牌的不銹鋼炊具組，給來會場最後一天的參觀者。

解析 本題屬於『複合形容詞』的綜合考法。由上下文句意判斷，動詞 (sell) 與名詞 (brand) 的關係應當是主動，又搭配形容詞加以修飾名詞，所以答案選 (C)。

超語感練習 🎧 Track 167

Every month, our magazine features a comparison of new cooking products available on the market; today, we are showing five of the top-selling brands of stainless steel cookware sets to our visitors on the last day of fair here.

18. The manager determined to lower the price for purchasers because wireless connectors are - - - - - - - - types of devices and choices for young novices and professional experts to operate electronics alike in seconds.

(A) prefers
(B) prefer
(C) preferring
(D) preferred

中譯 (D) 這位經理決定為買家降低價格，因為無線連接器，對年輕的新手和專業的專家而言，是首選的設備和選擇；對他們來說，可以在很短時間，操作類似的電子產品。

解析 本題屬於『過去分詞』的考法。由上下文結構判斷，空格雖然為「動詞」選項，但是因為用來修飾後面「名詞 (types)」，所以「動詞 (prefer)」變成「分詞 (preferred)」答案，中文翻譯為「較（被）喜歡的……」；且動詞與名詞的關係應該為「被動」用法，所以答案選 (D)。

超語感練習 **Track 168**

The manager determined to lower the price for purchasers because wireless connectors are preferred types of devices and choices for young novices and professional experts to operate electronics alike in seconds.

19. As a practitioner of cooking, I suggest our buyers to choose cookware that is constructed around a copper core, - - - - - - - - heat more evenly. And this feature cannot be stressed enough.

(A) distributing
(B) distributed
(C) distributes
(D) distribute

中譯 (A) 身為烹飪界的一員，我建議我們的消費者，要選擇沿著圍繞銅質中心打造、更均勻分佈熱量的炊具。而這個功能在怎麼強調也不為過。

解析 本題屬於『分詞構句』中的『現在分詞』考法。由上下文結構判斷，空格雖然為「動詞」選項，但是因為沒有「連接詞」，推測應當是省略「連接詞(which/that)」，所以選擇「動詞(distributes)」變成「分詞(distributing)」的答案；且動詞與主詞的關係應該為「主動」用法，所以答案選(A)。

超語感練習 🎧 Track 169

As a practitioner of cooking, I suggest our buyers to choose cookware that is constructed around a copper core, distributing heat more evenly. And this feature cannot be stressed enough.

20. As to the use of this machine, we strongly suggest users
- - - - - - - - prior working experience in the related fields of
publication are preferred but not required.
(A) equipping
(B) equipped
(C) equip
(D) equips

中譯 (A) 至於本機的使用，我們強烈建議，優先考慮具備相關領域工作經驗
的使用者，但這不是必備條件。

解析 本題屬於『現在分詞』的考法。由上下文結構判斷，空格雖然為「動
詞」選項，但是因為與前句並沒有「連接詞」存在，推測應當是省
略「連接詞(which/that)」，所以選擇「動詞(equip)」變成「分詞
(equipping)」的答案；且動詞與名詞的關係應該為「主動」用法，所
以答案選(A)。

超語感練習 Track 170

As to the use of this machine, we strongly suggest
users equipping prior working experience in the
related fields of publication are preferred but not
required.

21. Everyone at Sheerwood Furniture hopes that you - - - - - - - - be happy in your new occupation.

(A) will
(B) should
(C) would
(D) might

中譯 **(A)** 每位在 Sheerwood 傢俱行的人都希望你將會滿意你的新居住環境。

解析 hope「希望」，在未來達成的事，用 will「將會」，故選 (A)。選項 (B)、(C)、(D) 皆用在 wish「希望；但願」。例句：I hope that he will pass the driving test. 我希望他會通過駕駛考試。

 超語感練習 Track 171

Everyone at Sheerwood Furniture hopes that you will be happy in your new occupation.

22. Since the earliest twentieth century, - - - - - - - - from many countries have attempted to explore the underwater world around these islands.

(A) marines

(B) divers

(C) astronauts

(D) scientists

中譯 (B) 自二十世紀早期，各國潛水員試圖探索這些島附近的海底世界。

解析 此題為單字題，依照題意，應選擇選項 (B) 潛水員最為恰當。選項 (A) 為海軍陸戰隊隊員、選項 (C) 為太空人、選項 (D) 為科學家。

超語感練習 Track 172

Since the earliest twentieth century, divers from many countries have attempted to explore the underwater world around these islands.

23. Rarely has a fully intact dinosaur skeleton of this level of
- - - - - - - - been dug up anywhere in the world.

(A) conservation
(B) preservation
(C) maintenance
(D) upkeep

中譯 (B) 世界各地罕見這種完好無缺保存程度的恐龍骨骸。

解析 此題為單字題，4個選項皆為名詞，而依照題意，應選擇選項(B) 保存最為恰當。選項 (A) 為保護、選項 (C) 為維護、選項 (D) 為維修。

超語感練習 Track 173

Rarely has a fully intact dinosaur skeleton of this level of preservation been dug up anywhere in the world.

24. This year's annual conference could have been organized better if more members - - - - - - - - actively.

(A) would participate
(B) participate
(C) had participated
(D) were participated

中譯 (C) 如果有更多的成員積極參加的話，今年的年會將會組織安排地更好。

解析 本題考題屬於『假設語氣』考法中，與「過去時間」相反的假設。由句中連接詞 (if) 與動詞 (could have been organized) 判斷，空格的動詞應當用與「過去時間」相反的「過去完成式」；又由上下句意判斷，應該要用「主動」，所以答案選 (C)。

超語感練習  Track 174

This year's annual conference could have been organized better if more members had participated actively.

25. The guest speaker at the annual conference delivered an -------- speech which was much appreciated by all those present.

(A) inspiration
(B) inspire
(C) inspirational
(D) inspirationally

中譯　(C) 年度討論會的客座講者發表了激勵人心的演說，所有與會者皆十分欣賞。

解析　an inspirational speech「激勵人心的演說」是名詞片語，inspirational「激勵的」是形容詞，修飾名詞 speech「演說」。

超語感練習　🎧 Track 175

The guest speaker at the annual conference delivered an inspirational speech which was much appreciated by all those present.

26. I have seen one of your safes in a fair booth, you - - - - - - - - on your address to me.
(A) passing
(B) passed
(C) past
(D) passes

中譯 (A) 在你傳你的地址給我 (之前)，我在會展攤位看到你的保險箱之一。

解析 本題屬於『現在分詞』的考法。由上下文結構判斷，空格雖然為「動詞」選項，但是因為與前句並沒有「連接詞」存在，推測應當是省略「連接詞 (before)」，所以選擇「動詞」變成「分詞」的答案；且動詞 (pass) 與名詞 (you) 的關係應該為「主動」用法，用「現在分詞」形式當「形容詞」，是為「主動傳遞」的句意，所以答案選 (A)。

超語感練習 🎧 Track 176

I have seen one of your safes in a fair booth, you passing on your address to me.

27. Through our service, you can rent one of our five rooms
fully - - - - - - - - for business purposes.
(A) furnishes
(B) furnish
(C) furnished
(D) furnishing

中譯 (C) 通過我們的服務，你可以租我們五間設備齊全之一的房間，用於商
業目的。

解析 本題屬於『過去分詞』的考法。由上下文結構判斷，空格雖然為「動
詞」選項，但是因為與前句並沒有「連接詞」存在，推測應當是省略
「連接詞(which/that)」，所以選擇「動詞(is furnished)」變成「分詞
(furnished)」的答案；且動詞與名詞的關係應該為「被動」用法，所以
答案選(C)。

超語感練習 Track 177

Through our service, you can rent one of our five
rooms fully furnished for business purposes.

28. Alternatively, you will find a smaller size 11-inch laptop
-------- in our flagship store on Jiang-Kang Rd.

(A) showed
(B) show
(C) shows
(D) showing

中譯 (A) 另一個選擇是，你會在我們健康路旗艦店發現，有展示更小尺寸的
11英吋筆記型電腦。

解析 本題屬於『過去分詞』的考法。由上下文結構判斷，空格雖然為「動
詞」選項，但是因為與前句並沒有「連接詞」存在，推測應當是省略
「連接詞 (which/that)」，所以選擇「動詞 (is showed)」變成「分詞
(showed)」的答案；且動詞與名詞的關係應該為「被動」用法，所以
答案選 (A)。

超語感練習 Track 178

Alternatively, you will find a smaller size 11-inch
laptop showed in our flagship store on Jiang-Kang
Rd.

29. It would be of great help if you could demonstrate the operation process on the spot, - - - - - - - - the range of compatibility supplied as you guaranteed.

(A) proves
(B) prove
(C) proving
(D) proved

中譯 (C) 如果你能當場證明，在操作過程中，所提供的兼相容性範圍會如您保證，這將是很大的幫助。

解析 本題屬於『分詞構句』中的『現在分詞』考法。由上下文結構判斷，空格雖然為「動詞」選項，但是沒有「連接詞」存在，推測應當是省略「連接詞 (which/that)」，所以選擇「動詞 (proves)」變成「分詞 (proving)」的答案；且動詞與主詞的關係應該為「主動」用法，所以答案選 (C)。

超語感練習 🎧 Track 179

It would be of great help if you could demonstrate the operation process on the spot, proving the range of compatibility supplied as you guaranteed.

30. Come to our fair event you will know that our academic support office is ‑‑‑‑‑‑‑‑ on campus, while the research and marketing section are in the downtown complex building.

(A) locate
(B) locates
(C) locating
(D) located

中譯 **(D)** 來到我們展場，你將瞭解，我們的學術支援辦公室位於校園內，而研發和市場部都在市中心綜合大樓。

解析 本題屬於『過去分詞』的考法。由上下文結構判斷，空格雖然為「動詞」選項，但是因為與前句並沒有「連接詞」存在，推測應當是省略「連接詞 (which/that)」，所以選擇「動詞 (located)」變成「分詞 (located)」的答案；且動詞與名詞的關係應該為「被動」用法，所以答案選 (D)。

超語感練習  **Track 180**

Come to our fair event you will know that our academic support office is located on campus, while the research and marketing section are in the downtown complex building.

銀行金融

擬真試題

1. Many companies are still reluctant to make major capital investments out of uncertainty over - - - - - - - - the recovery will continue.

(A) so

(B) which

(C) that

(D) whether

中譯 (D) 許多公司仍然不願意，在復甦能否持續的不確定中，作出重大資本投資。

解析 本題屬於『連接詞』中的「名詞子句」考法。由上下文句意判斷，介系詞(over)後面應用「名詞子句」當受詞，又為「選擇性」句意，所以答案選(D)。

超語感練習　🎧 Track 181

Many companies are still reluctant to make major capital investments out of uncertainty over whether the recovery will continue.

Unit 1
Unit 2
Unit 3
Unit 4
Unit 5
Unit 6
Unit 7
Unit 8
Unit 9
Unit 10

2. This way, your monthly savings deposit takes a small contribution from every paycheck automatically, and you will be surprised - - - - - - - - quickly this simple trick can make your savings add up.

(A) what
(B) how
(C) why
(D) that

中譯 (B) 這樣一來，你每月的儲蓄存款會自動從每個月的薪水扣除，而且你會驚奇地發現，這個簡單的技巧可迅速地讓您的儲蓄增加。

解析 本題屬於『連接詞』中的「名詞子句」考法。由上下文句意判斷，形容詞 (surprised) 後面應用「名詞子句」結構，空格後面又為副詞 (quickly)，所以選擇承接「不完整句意」表示「方式、方法」的答案 (D)。

超語感練習  Track 182

This way, your monthly savings deposit takes a small contribution from every paycheck automatically, and you will be surprised that quickly this simple trick can make your savings add up.

3. The most attractive yet dangerous aspect of the credit system is that you can buy things - - - - - - -, at the moment, you do not have enough money.

(A) even if
(B) despite
(C) and
(D) which

中譯 (A) 信用體系最吸引人，但也是最危險的地方在於，就算那一刻你沒有足夠的錢，你還是可以買東西。

解析 本題屬於『連接詞』中的「副詞子句」考法。由上下文句意判斷，應該選擇「即使、雖然」句意的答案 (A)。

超語感練習 🎧 Track 183

The most attractive yet dangerous aspect of the credit system is that you can buy things even if, at the moment, you do not have enough money.

4. I am writing in reference to an overdue payment for invoice #5542-87, - - - - - - - - is now in excess of three months overdue.

(A) what
(B) that
(C) which
(D) who

中譯 (C) 這封信是要告知您，其中提到的逾期付款發票 # 5542-87，目前逾期超過三個月。

解析 本題屬於『連接詞』中的「形容詞子句」考法。由上下文句意判斷，空格前面的先行詞為非人 (payment)，且空格前有逗點 (,)，為「非限定用法」，且不可用 that，且空格後面為「動詞」，直接表示空格為關係代名詞的「主詞 (which)」用法，所以答案選 (C)。

超語感練習  Track 184

I am writing in reference to an overdue payment for invoice #5542-87, which is now in excess of three months overdue.

5. I appreciate a letter of apology from your department - - - - - - - - you have verified these errors made by your clients' account management.

(A) and

(B) no sooner than

(C) as soon as

(D) before

中譯 (C) 您於確認管理客戶帳戶時所犯得錯誤後，便立即自您部門發出的道歉信函，對此我很感激。

解析 本題屬於『連接詞』中的「副詞子句」考法。由上下文句意判斷，應該選擇「一……就……」句意的答案 (C)。而答案 (B) 錯在結構錯誤，所以不選。

超語感練習 🎧 Track 185

I appreciate a letter of apology from your department as soon as you have verified these errors made by your clients' account management.

6. Would you please arrange for $3,000, - - - - - - - - is to be transferred from our No. 2 account to their account with Denmark Banks, Leadshell Street, London, on the 1st of every month, beginning 1st May this year?

(A) but
(B) and
(C) which
(C) what

中譯 (C) 可否請您安排，從今年五月起，每個月的 1 號從我們的 2 號帳戶轉移 3000 美元到他們在倫敦 Leadshell 街丹麥銀行的帳戶？

解析 本題屬於『連接詞』中的「形容詞子句」考法。由上下文句意判斷，空格前面的先行詞為非人 ($3,000)，為「非限定用法」，空格後面為「動詞」，直接表示空格為關係代名詞的「主詞 (which)」用法，所以答案選 (C)。

超語感練習  Track 186

Would you please arrange for $3,000, which is to be transferred from our No. 2 account to their account with Denmark Banks, Leadshell Street, London, on the 1st of every month, beginning 1st May this year?

7. I am writing to you with reference to our conversation three days ago - - - - - - - - we discussed my opening a current account with your branch.

(A) what
(B) how
(C) when
(D) where

中譯 (C) 這封信是關於，三天前在談話中，討論到我在您們分行開立活期帳戶一事。

解析 本題屬於『連接詞』中的「副詞子句」考法。由上下文句意判斷，應該選擇與時間「當……時」相關的句意，所以答案選 (B)。

超語感練習 Track 187

I am writing to you with reference to our conversation three days ago when we discussed my opening a current account with your branch.

8. Our invoice clearly requested a full payment within 45 days of delivery, and this is the third reminder ------- we have sent you regarding this invoice.

(A) what
(B) of which
(C) which
(D) who

中譯 (C) 我們的發票明確要求，全額付款後 45 天交貨，而這是我們已經向您發出有關該發票的第三次提醒。

解析 本題屬於『連接詞』中的「形容詞子句」考法。由上下文句意判斷，空格前面的先行詞為非人 (reminder)，為「限定用法」，且與介系詞用法無關，且空格後面為「主詞」加「動詞」結構，直接表示空格為關係代名詞的「受詞」或「副詞」用法，所以答案選 (C)。

超語感練習　🎧 Track 188

Our invoice clearly requested a full payment within 45 days of delivery, and this is the third reminder which we have sent you regarding this invoice.

9. Will you please note that as from August 11th —the two signatures that will appear on the cheques for our number 1 and 2 accounts will be mine - - - - - - - - that of our new accountant Mr. Harolf, who is taking over from Mr. David?

(A) but
(B) and
(C) or
(C) what

中譯 (B) 可否請你注意，從 8 月 11 日起，兩個將出現在我們的 1 號和 2 帳戶支票上的簽名，一個名字是我，和我們即將接管 David 先生業務的新會計 Harolf 先生？

解析 本題屬於『連接詞』中的「對等連接詞」考法。由上下文句意判斷，後面應用「承接句意、前後一致」的連接詞，所以答案選 (B)。

超語感練習 Track 189

Will you please note that as from August 11th —the two signatures that will appear on the cheques for our number 1 and 2 accounts will be mine and that of our new accountant Mr. Harolf, who is taking over from Mr. David?

10. The account numbers and details are on the enclosed transfer slip, and I would be grateful - - - - - - - - you could stamp the counterfoil and return it to me.

(A) since
(B) because
(C) as
(D) if

中譯 (D) 該帳號的號碼及細節在附件裡的轉帳單上；如果你能加蓋存根，並將其返回的話，我將不勝感激。

解析 本題屬於『連接詞』中的「副詞子句」考法。由上下文句意判斷，應該選擇與條件「假如」相關的句意，所以答案選 (D)。

超語感練習 Track 190

The account numbers and details are on the enclosed transfer slip, and I would be grateful if you could stamp the counterfoil and return it to me.

11. Thank you for your letter of August 8th, and please allow me to apologize for my oversight in not realizing - - - - - - - - I had a debit balance on my current account.

(A) unless

(B) because

(C) which

(D) that

中譯 **(D)** 感謝您 8 月 8 日的來信，並請允許我對您致歉，因為我的疏忽，沒有意識到我目前的賬戶出現借方餘額。

解析 本題屬於『連接詞』中的「名詞子句」考法。由上下文句意判斷，動詞 (realize) 後面應用「名詞子句」當受詞的結構，所以選擇承接「完整句意」的答案 (D)。

超語感練習 🎧 Track 191

Thank you for your letter of August 8th, and please allow me to apologize for my oversight in not realizing that I had a debit balance on my current account.

12. With reference to our meeting on 23rd September, we are pleased to tell you that the credit for two million NT dollars, - - - - - - - - you requested has been approved.

(A) who
(B) so
(C) than
(D) which

中譯 (D) 參照本次 9 月 23 日的會議，我們很高興地告訴您，您所要求的信貸 200 萬台幣已被批准。

解析 本題屬於『連接詞』中的「形容詞子句」考法。由上下文句意判斷，空格前面的先行詞為非人 (two million NT dollars)，為「非限定用法」，且空格後面為「主詞」加「動詞」結構，直接表示空格為關係代名詞的「受詞」或「副詞」用法，所以答案選 (D)。

超語感練習 Track 192

With reference to our meeting on 23rd September, we are pleased to tell you that the credit for two million NT dollars, which you requested has been approved.

13. The money will be credited to your current account - - - - - - - -
available from September 30th subject to your returning
schedule by that time.

(A) and

(B) yet

(C) but

(D) for

中譯 (A) 這筆錢將存入您的當前帳戶，並從 9 月 30 日起入帳，而這件事可依您之後回程的行程作更改。

解析 本題屬於『連接詞』中的「對等連接詞」考法。由上下文句意判斷，後面應用「承接句意、前後一致」的連接詞，所以答案選 (A)。

超語感練習 🎧 Track 193

The money will be credited to your current account
and available from September 30th subject to your
returning schedule by that time.

14. -------- agreed, we have forwarded our bill, No. 1671 for $30,000 NT dollars with the documents to your bank, Nederlandsche Bank in Amsterdam.

(A) Though
(B) With
(C) As
(D) Despite

中譯 (C) 按照約定，我們轉發我們的帳款，編號 1671 號，總計 30,000 元台幣與文件，到您在阿姆斯特丹的 Nederlandsche Bank 銀行。

解析 本題屬於『連接詞』中的「副詞子句」考法。由上下文句意判斷，應該選擇與擬態「就如同……」相關的句意，所以答案選 (C)。

超語感練習  Track 194

As agreed we have forwarded our bill, No. 1671 for $30,000 NT dollars with the documents to your bank, Nederlandsche Bank in Amsterdam.

15. - - - - - - - - the account is still not settled, we will have to make a formal protest, which we hope will not be necessary.

(A) Unless
(B) Providing that
(C) Because
(D) Due to

中譯 (B) 假如該帳戶仍然沒有解決，我們將必須作出正式抗議，而我們希望這將可以避免。

解析 本題屬於『連接詞』中的「副詞子句」考法。由上下文句意判斷，應該選擇與假設「如果」相關的句意，所以答案選 (B)。

超語感練習 🎧 Track 195

Providing that the account is still not settled, we will have to make a formal protest, which we hope will not be necessary.

16. We have instructed our bank, Northern City Ltd., to open a confirmed irrevocable letter of credit for $3,500 US dollars in your favor, - - - - - - - - is valid until June 1st.

(A) which
(B) that
(C) whom
(D) who

中譯 (A) 我們已通知我方銀行 --Northern City 有限公司，開立以您為抬頭、3,500 美元的保兌不可撤銷信用狀，有效期至 6 月 1 日。

解析 本題屬於『連接詞』中的「形容詞子句」考法。由上下文句意判斷，空格前面的先行詞為非人 (letter of credit)，為「非限定用法」，且空格後面為「動詞」，直接表示空格為關係代名詞的「主詞 (which)」用法，且前面有逗點，所以答案選 (A)。

超語感練習 Track 196

We have instructed our bank, Northern City Ltd., to open a confirmed irrevocable letter of credit for $3,500 dollars in your favor, which is valid until June 1st.

17. I am writing to inform you - - - - - - - - you have an overdraft of NT$1,500 on your current account.

(A) though
(B) after
(C) that
(D) what

中譯　(C) 這封信是要告知您，您目前的帳戶有新台幣 1500 元的透支。

解析　本題屬於『連接詞』中的「名詞子句」考法。由上下文句意判斷，動詞 (inform) 後面應用「名詞子句」當受詞的結構，所以選擇承接「完整句意」的答案 (C)。

超語感練習　🎧 Track 197

I am writing to inform you that you have an overdraft of NT$1,500 on your current account.

18. The bank allowed your last credit transfer to Hank Ltd. to pass - - - - - - - - you have a large credit balance on your deposit account.

(A) as
(B) for
(C) after
(D) which

中譯 (A) 銀行允許您將最後的額度轉移到 Hank 有限公司；因為您的存款賬戶有大量的貸方餘額。

解析 本題屬於『連接詞』中的「副詞子句」考法。由上下文句意判斷，應該選擇與時間「當⋯⋯時」相關的句意，所以答案選 (A)。

超語感練習 Track 198

The bank allowed your last credit transfer to Hank Ltd. to pass as you have a large credit balance on your deposit account.

19. However, we would like to point out that we cannot allow overdraft facilities ------- you make a formal arrangement with the bank.

(A) thus
(B) unless
(C) as soon as
(D) the instant

中譯 (B) 不過，我們要指出，除非你與銀行有正式的安排，否則我們無法允許透支。

解析 本題屬於『連接詞』中的「副詞子句」考法。由上下文句意判斷，應該選擇與假設「除非」相關的句意，所以答案選 (D)。

超語感練習 Track 199

However, we would like to point out that we cannot allow overdraft facilities unless you make a formal arrangement with the bank.

20. Thank you for allowing the credit transfer to Homemakers to go through - - - - - - - - the fact that it created the debit balance.

(A) as if
(B) though
(C) in spite
(D) despite

中譯 (D) 謝謝你將信貸轉讓給 Homemaker 以利週轉，儘管它已產生借方餘額的事實。

解析 本題屬於『連接詞』中的「副詞子句」考法。由上下文句意判斷，應該選擇與讓步「即使、雖然」相關的句意，且後面用「名詞」與「名詞子句」的「同位語關係」，所以答案選「介系詞」＋「名詞」的結構，所以選 (D)。選項 (C) 應該為 in spite of ＋ N 或 in spite that ＋ 子句用法，因為與文法不符，所以不選。

超語感練習  Track 200

Thank you for allowing the credit transfer to Homemakers to go through despite the fact that it created the debit balance.

21. Judy would like to make an appointment to see you in order - - - - - - - - she tends to discuss either a loan or overdraft to enable her to expand her business.

(A) to
(B) that
(C) which
(D) for

中譯　(B) Judy 想與你約時間碰面，因為她想與你討論貸款或透支的問題，使她能夠拓展自己的業務。

解析　本題屬於『連接詞』中的「副詞子句」考法。由上下文句意判斷，應該選擇與目的「為了要……」相關的句意，且要用「連接詞」結構，所以答案選 (B)。

超語感練習　Track 201

Judy would like to make an appointment to see you in order that she tends to discuss either a loan or overdraft to enable her to expand her business.

22. Due to the high volume of - - - - - - - - to our website, transactions are taking longer than usual to process.

(A) vehicles

(B) trucks

(C) traffic

(D) carriers

中譯 (C) 由於我們網站的高流量，交易過程會比平常的處理時間長。

解析 此題為單字題，依照題意應選選項 (C) traffic「交通、流量」等意。而選項 (A) 為車輛、選項 (B) 為卡車、而選項 (D) 為置物架。

超語感練習 Track 202

Due to the high volume of traffic to our website, transactions are taking longer than usual to process.

23. Delta Data Services - - - - - - - - beat investor expectations in the second quarter.

(A) comfort
(B) comfortable
(C) comfortably
(D) comforted

中譯 (C) Delta 資料服務安逸地勝過投資者在第二季的預期。

解析 句中空格後的 beat 為動詞，以副詞修飾動詞，故選 (C)，以副詞 comfortably「安逸地」修飾動詞 beat「勝過」。選項 (A) 為安逸（名詞）；選項 (B) 為安逸的（形容詞）；選項 (D) 為安慰（過去式動詞）。

超語感練習  Track 203

Delta Data Services comfortably beat investor expectations in the second quarter.

24. - - - - - - - - to pay this bill on time may lead to a penalty or to the disconnection of your telephone.

(A) Failure
(B) To fail
(C) Fail
(D) Failed

中譯 (A) 不履行準時付這個帳單，會導致罰款或切斷電話線。

解析 "to pay"「付」，是不定詞作形容詞，形容詞修飾名詞，所以需要一個名詞，故選 (A) 失敗。而選項 (B) 為不定詞、選項 (C) 為動詞、而選項 (D) 則為形容詞。

超語感練習  Track 204

Failure to pay this bill on time may lead to a penalty or to the disconnection of your telephone.

25. It is rumored that the discount that is - - - - - - - - offered to new customers will be discontinued.
(A) rarely
(B) recently
(C) usually
(D) equally

中譯 (C) 傳言說通常提供給新顧客的折扣將不會繼續。

解析 句中的 be offered to 是「被提供給……」的意思，所以 offered 在這裡為動詞的被動型態，空格中應填入副詞來修飾動詞 offered，但 4 格選項皆為副詞，故依題意選擇 (C)usually 通常地。選項 (A) 為很少地、選項 (B) 為最近地、選項 (D) 為相當地。

超語感練習 Track 205

It is rumored that the discount that is usually offered to new customers will be discontinued.

26. The newspaper reported that the billionaire gave all his money - - - - - - - - before he passed away.
(A) up
(B) in
(C) away
(D) from

中譯 (C) 報紙報導億萬富翁捐出他所有的錢，在他過世之前。

解析 give ＋名詞＋away＝give＋away＋名詞。away是副詞；give away「贈送；捐贈」。(A)give up「放棄」。(B)give in「讓步」。(D) give from 沒有任何意思。例句：Wendy gave her old clothes away before Chinese New Year.＝Wendy gave her old clothes away before Chinese New Year.（Wendy在農曆新年之前把她的舊衣服捐贈出去。）

超語感練習 🎧 **Track 206**

The newspaper reported that the billionaire gave all his money away before he passed away.

27. Regulators have made the bank - - - - - - - to all customers who were mis-sold investment accounts.

(A) apology
(B) apologize
(C) apologetic
(D) to apologize

中譯 **(B)** 調解會迫使銀行向所有投資帳戶被誤賣掉的顧客道歉。

解析 make 是不完全及物動詞，需要一個受詞補語在受詞 the bank「銀行」的後面，受詞補語是原形動詞，故選 (B)。例句：The doctor made the sick boy take medicine.（醫生迫使生病的男孩吃藥。）

超語感練習 🎧 Track 207

Regulators have made the bank apologize to all customers who were mis-sold investment accounts.

28. The latest release of data has shown that growth in export markets has helped Germany avoid the expected - - - - - - - -.
(A) regression
(B) receding
(C) retreat
(D) recession

中譯 (D) 最近發佈的資料顯示，輸出市場幫助德國避免預期的衰退。

解析 此題為單字題，依照題意，應該選擇選項 (D) 衰退最為恰當。其他選項單字中文解釋則分別為 (A) 退化、(B) 退去、及 (C) 撤退。

超語感練習 Track 208

The latest release of data has shown that growth in export markets has helped Germany avoid the expected recession.

29. We are prepared to allow you a further three days before presenting it to the bank again, - - - - - - - - time we hope that the draft will have been met.

(A) in which
(B) which
(C) on which
(D) for which

中譯 (A) 我們準備再寬限您三天時間，以便您再次將款項存入銀行，而這一次我們希望該匯票將會兌現。

解析 本題屬於『連接詞』中的「形容詞子句」考法。由上下文句意判斷，空格前面的先行詞為非人 (three days)，為「限定用法」，且空格後面為「主詞」加「動詞」結構，直接表示空格為關係代名詞的「受詞」或「副詞」用法；且句中缺少與「先行詞」相搭配的「介系詞」用法，所以答案選 (A)。

超語感練習 🎧 Track 209

We are prepared to allow you a further three days before presenting it to the bank again, in which time we hope that the draft will have been met.

30. There is also a credit squeeze at present - - - - - - - - has particularly affected loans to the service sector of the economy.

(A) who

(B) so

(C) what

(D) which

中譯 (D) 在經濟上對服務業而言，目前還有一個會特別影響貸款的信貸緊縮。

解析 本題屬於『連接詞』中的「形容詞子句」考法。由上下文句意判斷，空格前面的先行詞為非人 (credit squeeze)，為「限定用法」，且空格後面為「動詞」，直接表示空格為關係代名詞的「主詞 (which)」用法，所以答案選 (D)。

超語感練習 Track 210

There is also a credit squeeze at present which has particularly affected loans to the service sector of the economy.

擬真試題

1. A copy of our prospectus containing particulars of our policies - - - - - - - - householders is enclosed.

(A) for

(B) of

(C) at

(D) by

中譯 (A) 附件是我們計畫書的副本，上有包含我們房屋所有人的保單詳情。

解析 本題考題屬於『介系詞』考法中「介系詞＋名詞」的考法。從上下文句意判斷，介系詞的中文翻譯為「為了……」，所以答案選 (A)。

超語感練習  Track 211

A copy of our prospectus containing particulars of our policies for householders is enclosed.

2. Consequently, we are prepared to offer you a total of £4,800 in full compensation - - - - - - - - your policy.

(A) by
(B) in
(C) under
(D) between

中譯 (C) 因此，我們準備為您提供，在您的保單下，共計 4,800 英鎊的全額賠償。

解析 本題考題屬於『介系詞』考法中「介系詞＋名詞」的考法。從上下文句意判斷，介系詞的中文翻譯為「在……之下」，所以答案選 (C)。

超語感練習 Track 212

Consequently, we are prepared to offer you a total of £4,800 in full compensation under your policy.

3. As you propose to ship regularly, we can offer you a rate of 2.48% benefit interest - - - - - - - - a total cover of £60,000.

(A) for
(B) of
(C) with
(D) from

中譯　(A) 就你提出定期出貨的建議，我們可提供您總計 60,000 英鎊的保障與 $ 2.48% 的利率優惠。

解析　本題考題屬於『介系詞』考法中「介系詞＋名詞」的考法。從上下文句意判斷，介系詞的中文翻譯為「總計……」，所以答案選 (A)。

超語感練習　🎧 Track 213

As you propose to ship regularly, we can offer you a rate of 2.48% benefit interest for a total cover of £60,000.

4. In particular we wish to know whether you can give a special rate - - - - - - - - return for the promise of regular monthly shipments.

    (A) in
    (B) for
    (C) by
    (D) against

中譯 (A) 我們特別想知道，你是否可因每月定期運送貨物的承諾，給一個優惠的價格當作回饋。

解析 本題考題屬於『介系詞』考法中「介系詞＋名詞」的考法。從上下文句意判斷，介系詞的中文翻譯為「回應/回覆……」，所以答案選(A)。

超語感練習  Track 214

In particular we wish to know whether you can give a special rate in return for the promise of regular monthly shipments.

5. The personal medical insurance will be effective - - - - - - - -
our receiving the enclosed proposal form which is
completed by you.
(A) with
(B) on
(C) within
(D) at

中譯　(B) 當我們一收到你所完成的附件申請表，個人醫療保險將生效。

解析　本題考題屬於『介系詞』考法中「介系詞＋名詞」的考法。從上下文句
意判斷，介系詞的中文翻譯為「一……就……」的句意，所以答案選
(B)。

超語感練習　🎧 Track 215

The personal medical insurance will be effective on
our receiving the enclosed proposal form which is
completed by you.

6. Please send me particulars of your terms and conditions
- - - - - - - - the policy and a proposal form if required.
(A) with
(B) on
(C) for
(D) at

中譯 (C) 如果需要的話,請給我你的保單條款、條件與申請表格的詳情。

解析 本題考題屬於『介系詞』考法中「介系詞+名詞」的考法。從上下文句意判斷,介系詞的中文翻譯為「為了……」,所以答案選 (C)。

超語感練習  Track 216

Please send me particulars of your terms and
conditions for the policy and a proposal form if
required.

7. Doctors believe that the calories you --------- could affect many aspects of your health.

(A) consume
(B) assume
(C) presume
(D) contract

中譯 (A) 醫生們相信你吃進的熱量可能會影響到健康許多面向。

解析 此題為單字題，依照題意，應該選擇選項 (A) 攝取最為恰當。其他選項單字中文解釋則分別為 (B) 以為、(C) 假定、及 (D) 訂合約。

超語感練習 Track 217

Doctors believe that the calories you consume could affect many aspects of your health.

8. Little is known about where the next outbreak will take place, but doctors in many countries are on - - - - - - - -.
(A) stand down
(B) stand up
(C) standby
(D) stand off

中譯 (C) 雖然不太知道下一次會在哪裡暴發，但是許多國家的醫生都在待命中。

解析 此題為單字題，依照題意，應該選擇選項 (C) 待命最為恰當。其他選項單字中文解釋則分別為 (A) 退出、(B) 起立、及 (D) 避開。

超語感練習  Track 218

Little is known about where the next outbreak will take place, but doctors in many countries are on standby.

9. From the copy of the report enclosed, one will see that although Jason agrees that the fire was probably caused by an electrical fault, he feels that £4,000 is a more likely evaluation for damage to stock - - - - - - - - present market prices.

(A) in
(B) at
(C) on
(D) with

中譯 (B) 我們從附上的報告副本裡知道，雖然 Jason 同意火災可能是由於電氣故障所造成，然而對於貨物存放災害的評估，他覺得 4000 英鎊約莫是目前的市場行情。

解析 本題考題屬於『介系詞』考法中「介系詞＋名詞」的考法。從上下文句意判斷，關鍵字為 price，片語的中文翻譯為「以⋯⋯價格」，所以答案選 (B)。

超語感練習 🎧 Track 219

From the copy of the report enclosed, one will see that although Jason agrees that the fire was probably caused by an electrical fault, he feels that £4,000 is a more likely evaluation for damage to stock at present market prices.

10. Further to our telephone conversation, I should be obliged for the details if you would review the rate of premium charged -------- the above fire policy for goods in our transit shed at No. 4 Dock.

(A) under
(B) at
(C) within
(D) with

中譯 **(A)** 另外在我們的電話交談中，假如你要檢查，在貨物火險下，4 號船塢轉運棚所收取的保費利率，我覺得我有責任解釋細節。

解析 本題考題屬於『介系詞』考法中「介系詞＋名詞」的考法。從上下文句意判斷，介系詞的中文翻譯為「在……(條件之下)」，所以答案選 (A)。

超語感練習  Track 220

Further to our telephone conversation, I should be obliged for the details if you would review the rate of premium charged under the above fire policy for goods in our transit shed at No. 4 Dock.

11. I have enclosed leaflets explaining our three fully-comprehensive industrial policies which offer the sort of cover you require, and I think that policy A351 would probably suit you best as it offers the widest protection - - - - - - - - 65% with full indemnification.

(A) in
(B) at
(C) on
(D) with

中譯　(B) 我已經隨信附上傳單，解釋我們三個全面廣泛的工業政策，提供您需要的承保內容。而我個人覺得，保單 A351 可能會最適合你，因為它提供 65% 全數理賠最廣泛的保護。

解析　本題考題屬於『介系詞』考法中「介系詞＋名詞」的考法。從上下文句意判斷，介系詞的中文翻譯為「以……（數字 / 差距）」，所以答案選 (B)。

超語感練習　🎧 Track 221

I have enclosed leaflets explaining our three fully-comprehensive industrial policies which offer the sort of cover you require, and I think that policy A351 would probably suit you best as it offers the widest protection at 65% with full indemnification.

12. I have recently bought the property at the above address with possession as off July 1st, and wish to take out comprehensive cover - - - - - - - - both building and contents in the sums of £120,000 and £30,000 respectively.

(A) in
(B) at
(C) on
(D) with

中譯 (C) 自 7 月 1 日起，我最近買了以上地址的房地產與地上所有物，並想對建物及內含物，分別保 120,000 英鎊與 30,000 英鎊的綜合型保單。

解析 本題考題屬於『介系詞』考法中「介系詞＋名詞」的考法。從上下文句意判斷，介系詞的中文翻譯為「專門對……」，所以答案選 (C)。

超語感練習 🎧 **Track 222**

I have recently bought the property at the above address with possession as off July 1st, and wish to take out comprehensive cover on both building and contents in the sums of £120,000 and £30,000 respectively.

13. I hope you will agree to reduce the coverage sufficiently to bring it more into line - - - - - - - - the extent of the risk insured under other policies.

(A) in
(B) at
(C) on
(D) with

中譯 **(D)** 我希望你能同意，將承保範圍壓低到與其他保單所保障的風險程度一致。

解析 本題考題屬於『介系詞』考法中「介系詞＋名詞」的考法。從上下文句意判斷，片語的中文翻譯為「與……一致 (bring sb/sth into line with)」，所以答案選 (D)。

超語感練習 Track 223

I hope you will agree to reduce the coverage sufficiently to bring it more into line with the extent of the risk insured under other policies.

14. - - - - - - - - reply to your letter of March 5th, I am pleased to say that arrangement for an all risk open cover policy for chinaware shipment to North and South American seaboard ports is granted.

(A) In
(B) At
(C) On
(D) With

中譯　(A) 回應您 3 月 5 日的來信中，我很高興地說，運往北美和南美沿海港口的瓷器中，所投保的預約保險單已經通過。

解析　本題考題屬於『介系詞』考法中「介系詞＋名詞」的考法。從上下文句意判斷，片語的中文翻譯為「回應／覆⋯⋯(in reply to...)」，所以答案選 (A)。

超語感練習　Track 224

In reply to your letter of March 5th, I am pleased to say that arrangement for an all risk open cover policy for chinaware shipment to North and South American seaboard ports is granted.

15. - - - - - - - - this situation, we have been reluctantly compelled to introduce the medical insurances which have an automatic increase in the amount of premium at each renewal of the policy.

(A) In
(B) At
(C) On
(D) With

中譯 (A) 在這種情況下，我們不願意地被迫引進這種在每次保單展延時，將自動增加保費的醫療保險。

解析 本題考題屬於『介系詞』考法中「介系詞＋名詞」的考法。從上下文句意判斷，片語的中文翻譯為「在……情況 (in the situation...)」，所以答案選 (A)。

超語感練習 🎧 Track 225

In this situation, we have been reluctantly compelled to introduce the medical insurances which have an automatic increase in the amount of premium at each renewal of the policy.

16. Please confirm that you have arranged for this, and send me the customary endorsement indicating the charge - - - - - - - - inclusion in the policy schedule.

(A) for
(B) by
(C) on
(D) with

中譯　(A) 請確認您已安排了這一點後，將慣例的簽署內容寄給我，並於上方標示保單計畫的費用。

解析　本題考題屬於『介系詞』考法中「名詞＋介系詞」的考法。從上下文句意判斷，介系詞的中文翻譯為「為了……」，所以答案選 (A)。

超語感練習  Track 226

Please confirm that you have arranged for this, and send me the customary endorsement indicating the charge for inclusion in the policy schedule.

17. Unfortunately, our efforts to encourage medical policy-holders to take account - - - - - - - - revising the insured sums due to the inflation have been poorly supported.

(A) for
(B) at
(C) on
(D) of

中譯 (D) 不幸的是，我們努力於鼓勵醫療保戶投保人，因應通貨膨脹，而考慮修改被保險總額的這件事，不獲得支持。

解析 本題考題屬於『介系詞』考法中「動詞＋名詞＋介系詞」的考法。從上下文句意判斷，片語的中文翻譯為「把……列入考慮 (take account of…)」，所以答案選 (D)。

超語感練習 🎧 Track 227

unfortunately, our efforts to encourage medical policy-holders to take account of revising the insured sums due to the inflation have been poorly supported.

18. As to the estate insurance, the building we occupy belongs to us and is valued, along ------- the fixtures and fittings, at £250,000, and at any one time there might be stock worth £70,000 on the premises.

(A) in
(B) at
(C) on
(D) with

中譯 (D) 至於地產保險，我們所使用的這座建築是我們所有，連同設備及裝置，總價值 25 萬英鎊；以及無論何時，存放在這棟建築物裡，價值 70000 英鎊的物品。

解析 本題考題屬於『介系詞』考法中「形容詞＋名詞」的考法。從上下文句意判斷，片語的中文翻譯為「連同……(along with)」，所以答案選 (D)。

 **超語感練習** Track 228

As to the estate insurance, the building we occupy belongs to us and is valued, along with the fixtures and fittings, at £250,000, and at any one time there might be stock worth £70,000 on the premises.

19. The state saw recreational drug use - - - - - - - - after decriminalization last year.

(A) increasing
(B) increase
(C) increased
(D) to increase

中譯 (B) 政府發現用於娛樂消遣的藥物使用，在去年合法化之後增加。

解析 see 是及物動詞，受詞為名詞片語 recreational drug use「娛樂消遣的藥物使用」，後面需要一個受詞補語，受詞補語是原形動詞，故選 (B)。要注意，drug use 是名詞。例句：The interviewer saw an enormous cockroach crawl on the carpet during the interview. （面試官在面試期間看見一隻偌大的蟑螂爬在地毯上。）

超語感練習 🎧 Track 229

The state saw recreational drug use increase after
decriminalization last year.

20. When it opens, the new children's hospital ------- a level of care greater than that offered at any other hospital in the region.
(A) will provide
(B) provides
(C) has provided
(D) is providing

中譯 **(A)** 當它開始營業時，新的兒童醫院將會提供比該區任何其它醫院更好程度的照護。

解析 When it opens「當開始營業時」，表示事情仍未發生，是未來式，故選擇 (A)。動詞 provide「提供」。

超語感練習 Track 230

When it opens, the new children's hospital will provide a level of care greater than that offered at any other hospital in the region.

21. It has been shown that alcohol becomes - - - - - - - to health when consumed in large amounts.

(A) harm

(B) harmful

(C) harmfully

(D) harmed

中譯 (B) 攝取大量酒精被顯示已成為傷害健康的因素。

解析 become「成為」，是連綴動詞，所以後面要加主詞補語，連綴動詞的用法跟 be 動詞相同，本題適用的答案為一個形容詞，故選 (B)。例句：She has become depressed since she heard the bad news. 自從她聽到惡耗，她變得憂鬱。

超語感練習 🎧 Track 231

It has been shown that alcohol becomes harmful to health when consumed in large amounts.

22. All customers of Steve's Bar and Grill are kindly asked to refrain - - - - - - - - smoking on the open air terrace which overlooks the gardens.

(A) in
(B) off
(C) out
(D) from

中譯 (D) 所有 Steve's 酒吧與燒烤的顧客，被柔性勸導避免在俯瞰花園的開放陽台抽煙。

解析 此題為片語題型，refrain from「避免」。

超語感練習  Track 232

All customers of Steve's Bar and Grill are kindly asked to refrain from smoking on the open air terrace which overlooks the gardens.

23. Antibiotics are an essential component of every hospital's armory; however, - - - - - - - - effectiveness is being increasingly compromised by overuse.

(A) it

(B) theirs

(C) itself

(D) their

中譯 (D) 抗生素是每間醫院藥庫裡一項重要的成分；然而它的效用有增加過度使用的危險。

解析 代名詞所有格 their「他們的」，代表 antibiotics「抗生素」。

超語感練習 🎧 Track 233

Antibiotics are an essential component of every hospital's armory; however, their effectiveness is being increasingly compromised by overuse.

24. Extra insurance should be - - - - - - - - out by all those who plan to participate in the snowboarding activity.

(A) took
(B) take
(C) taken
(D) taking

中譯 (C) 額外的保險應該要從那些計畫參加滑板滑雪活動的人扣除。

解析 take out「扣除」，主詞是 extra insurance「額外的保險」，本句是被動語態。被動語態是主詞＋be 動詞＋過去分詞。例句：The cub should be taken away from its mother.（幼獸應該被帶離牠的母親。）

超語感練習 🎧 Track 234

Extra insurance should be taken out by all those who plan to participate in the snowboarding activity.

25. Farmers around the world are growing more and more
------- fruits and vegetables in order to meet growing
consumer demand.

(A) fresh
(B) whole
(C) healthy
(D) organic

中譯 (D) 世界各地的農夫正種植愈來愈多的有機的水果與蔬菜，以迎接日益
成長的消費者需求。

解析 本題為單字題型，選項 (A) 為新鮮的、選項 (B) 為完整的、選項 (C) 為健
康的，依題意選擇 (D) 有機的。

超語感練習 Track 235

Farmers around the world are growing more and
more organic fruits and vegetables in order to meet
growing consumer demand.

26. The accident at the construction site was very serious; however, all the injured are expected to make a full
- - - - - - - -.

(A) recover
(B) recovered
(C) recovery
(D) recovering

中譯 (C) 建築工地的事故十分嚴重，然而期待所有受傷的人完全復元。

解析 "full"「完全的」，是形容詞，後面必須是名詞。選項 (A) 為動詞、選項 (B) 為過去分詞、選項 (D) 為現在分詞。選項 (C) 為名詞，為正確答案。

超語感練習  Track 236

The accident at the construction site was very serious; however, all the injured are expected to make a full recovery.

27. New research has shown that habitat destruction has affected the - - - - - - - - in the area, but less than expected.

(A) nature
(B) culture
(C) wilderness
(D) wildlife

中譯 **(D)** 新研究顯示動物棲息地破壞影響了該區的野生生物，但影響程度不如預期大。

解析 本題為單字題型，選項 (A) 為自然、選項 (B) 為文化、選項 (C) 為荒野，依題意選擇 (D) 野生生物。

超語感練習 🎧 Track 237

New research has shown that habitat destruction has affected the wildlife in the area, but less than expected.

28. Although great effort was made to stop people lighting fires in the protected area, - - - - - - - success was very disappointing.

(A) their
(B) theirs
(C) its
(D) they

中譯 (C) 雖然已做出極大努力來停止人在保護區點火，但它的成效十分令人失望。

解析 its 是所有格形容詞，代表句子裡的主詞 great effort。

超語感練習 Track 238

Although great effort was made to stop people lighting fires in the protected area, its success was very disappointing.

29. The recent increase in visitor numbers to National Parks has caused - - - - - - - - damage to many pathways.

(A) unexpected

(B) undiscovered

(C) unexplained

(D) unauthorized

中譯 (A) 近期增加的國家公園遊客,已經對許多小徑造成意想不到的損傷。

解析 本題為單字題型,選項(B)為未發掘的、選項(C)為未經說明的、選項(D)為未授權的,依題意選擇(A)意想不到的。

超語感練習 Track 239

The recent increase in visitor numbers to National Parks has caused unexpected damage to many pathways.

30. Typhoon is a/an - - - - - - - - occurrence in the western Pacific from June to November each year.

(A) common
(B) often
(C) extraordinary
(D) unnatural

中譯 (A) 颱風是普遍發生在西太平洋的一種現象，約在每年的六月至十一月間。

解析 必須選擇形容詞，修飾名詞 occurrence「發生」。句中提到時間為「每年從六月至十一月間」，足以得知是為常態，故選 (A)。

超語感練習 Track 240

Typhoon is a common occurrence in the western Pacific from June to November each year.

擬真試題

1. A fully functional version of the program is made - - - - - - - - the exe files at no cost from the Internet for a 30 day evaluation.

(A) be downloaded
(B) to download
(C) to be downloaded
(D) downloaded

中譯 (B) 該計劃的全功能版本需從網路免費下載 exe 文件，並有 30 天的免費評估時間。

解析 本題屬於『被動式』中「使役動詞」的被動考法。由前面動詞（使役動詞）的被動式判斷，後面的動詞變化應該用 to VR 的變化，中文翻成「被下載……」。所以答案選 (B)。

超語感練習 🎧 Track 241

A fully functional version of the program is made to download the exe files at no cost from the Internet for a 30 day evaluation.

2. Aside from the unbearably high temperatures, global warming is also - - - - - - - - for the power to go out.

(A) blamed

(B) to be blamed

(C) blame

(D) to blame

中譯 (D) 除了難耐的高溫之外，全球暖化也導致能源的流失。

解析 本題屬於『被動式』中「blame」的被動考法。由上下文的句意判斷，後面的動詞變化應該用 to VR 的變化來表示「被動」的意涵，中文翻成「為……負責」。所以答案選 (D)。

超語感練習  Track 242

Aside from the unbearably high temperatures, global warming is also to blame for the power to go out.

3. Due to technical problems, our website and mailbox for submission - - - - - - - - to be inaccessible for an indeterminate delay.

(A) are convinced
(B) convinced
(C) are convincing
(D) convincing

中譯　(A) 由於技術問題，我們的網站和交付的郵件信箱因為不明原因的延遲，確定是無法進入的。

解析　本題屬於『被動式』中「convince」的被動考法。由上下文的句意判斷，應當用「被動式」，中文翻成「被相信……」。所以答案選 (C)。

超語感練習　🎧 Track 243

Due to technical problems, our website and mailbox for submission are convincing to be inaccessible for an indeterminate delay.

4. In order to finish the file attachment process, a click on the attach button - - - - - - - - to be a must.

(A) is considered
(B) is considering
(C) considered
(D) considering

中譯 (A) 為了完成文件附加的過程，對附件按鈕點擊被認為是必須的。

解析 本題屬於『被動式』中「consider」的被動考法。由上下文的句意判斷，應當用「被動式」，中文翻成「被認為是⋯⋯」。所以答案選 (A)。

超語感練習 Track 244

In order to finish the file attachment process, a click on the attach button is considered to be a must.

5. It is our pleasure to announce that a new campus e-mail program was created recently, and its headquarters - - - - - - - - in the main building.

(A) was locating
(B) was to locate
(C) located
(D) was located

中譯 (D) 我們的榮幸地宣布，新校區的電子郵件程式最近被創立，而它的總部是設在主要大樓。

解析 本題屬於『被動式』中「locate」的被動考法。由上下文的句意判斷，應當用「被動式」，中文翻成「座落於……」。所以答案選 (D)。

超語感練習 🎧 Track 245

It is our pleasure to announce that a new campus e-mail program was created recently, and its headquarters was located in the main building.

6. Keeping up with current innovations and new, emerging services in information technology at the same time seems to be a nearly impossible task to - - - - - - - - with.

(A) get acquainted
(B) acquainted
(C) get acquainting
(D) acquainting

中譯 (A) 要同時熟悉、跟上當前的創新與新興的資科服務，這似乎是一個幾近於不可能達成的任務。

解析 本題屬於『被動式』中「blame」的被動考法。由上下文的句意判斷，後面的動詞變化應該用 get + V-p.p. 的變化來表示「被動」的意涵，中文翻成「對……熟悉」。所以答案選 (A)。

超語感練習  **Track 246**

Keeping up with current innovations and new, emerging services in information technology at the same time seems to be a nearly impossible task to get acquainted with.

7. Maintaining relationships with local businesses and industries has - - - - - - - - as something vital to promoting online career and technical education program certification.

(A) to know
(B) been known
(C) to be known
(D) known

中譯　(B) 對促進線上職業與技術教育課程的認證來說，保持與當地企業和商家的關係，一直被當作是十分重要的事。

解析　本題屬於『被動式』中「know」的被動考法。由前面結構 (has) 判斷，後面的動詞變化應該用 V-p.p. 的「完成式」變化；又由上下文的句意判斷，應當用「被動式」，中文翻成「被廣為人知的……」。所以答案選 (B)。

超語感練習　🎧 Track 247

Maintaining relationships with local businesses and industries has been known as something vital to promoting online career and technical education program certification.

8. Our customers - - - - - - - - at the fact that most of our recent e-mails were lost when the company's server crashed Wednesday morning.

(A) disappointed
(B) to be disappointed
(C) are disappointed
(D) are disappointing

中譯 (C) 令我們的客戶失望的是，當公司的伺服器週三上午當機時，絕大部分我們最近的郵件遺失了。

解析 本題屬於『被動式』中「disappoint」的被動考法。由前面結構（主詞）判斷，後面應該使用「動詞」，且搭配 disappoint 動詞的變化應該用 V-p.p. 的變化，中文翻成「覺得失望的⋯⋯」。所以答案選 (C)。

超語感練習　Track 248

Our customers are disappointed at the fact that most of our recent e-mails were lost when the company's server crashed Wednesday morning.

9. Our website has ------- capable of attracting and retaining profitable customer relationships.
(A) to be proving
(B) to be proved
(C) been proved
(D) proved

中譯 (C) 我們的網站已被證明，能夠吸引與留住有增值潛力的客戶關係。

解析 本題屬於『被動式』中「prove」的被動考法。由前面結構 (完成式 has) 判斷，後面的動詞變化應該用 V-p.p. 的「完成式」變化；又由上下文的句意判斷，應當用「被動式」，中文翻成「被證明的……」。所以答案選 (C)。

超語感練習　Track 249

Our website has been proved capable of attracting
and retaining profitable customer relationships.

10. The fingerprint recognition - - - - - - - - something the most affordable and cost effective compared to voice, retina and hand signature system.

(A) is made into
(B) is made of
(C) is made from
(D) is made

中譯 (A) 與聲音、視網膜和手工簽名的系統相比之下,指紋識別被塑造成最實惠和具有成本效益。

解析 本題屬於『被動式』中「make」的被動考法。由前面結構(主詞)判斷,後面的動詞變化應該用被動式(beV + V-p.p.);又由上下文的句意判斷,應當用「介系詞(into)」,中文翻成「變成……」。所以答案選(A)。

超語感練習  Track 250

The fingerprint recognition is made into something the most affordable and cost effective compared to voice, retina and hand signature system.

11. By regularly updating your computer, attackers are left
- - - - - - - - from being able to take advantage of software
flaws that they could otherwise use to break into your
system.

(A) blocked
(B) to block
(C) to be blocked
(D) block

中譯 (A) 定期更新您的電腦可阻止攻擊者利用軟體漏洞入侵您的電腦。

解析 本題屬於『被動式』中「使役動詞 (leave)」的被動考法。由前面結構
（動詞 left）與句意判斷，後面的動詞變化應該用被動式 (V-p.p.) 當作
「形容詞」使用，中文翻成「被阻擋的……」。所以答案選 (A)。

超語感練習 Track 251

By regularly updating your computer, attackers
are left blocked from being able to take advantage of
software flaws that they could otherwise use to break
into your system.

12. For those having difficulties viewing the page, we suggest you close your browsers, deleting all temporary internet files and then have the page - - - - - - - -.

(A) be reloaded
(B) to reload
(C) to be reloaded
(D) reloaded

中譯 (D) 對那些無法開啟頁面的人而言，我們建議你關閉瀏覽器，並刪除所有臨時的網路文件，然後將頁面重新載入。

解析 本題屬於『被動式』中「使役動詞 (have)」的被動考法。由前面結構 (have ＋非人的受詞) 與句意判斷，後面的動詞變化應該用被動式 (V-p. p.)，中文翻成「被重新載入」。所以答案選 (D)。

超語感練習 Track 252

For those having difficulties viewing the page, we suggest you close your browsers, deleting all temporary internet files and then have the page reloaded.

13. On the other hand, in a recent survey on online classes, 65% of 900 university students said they still - - - - - - - - no on-campus classes, because of the face to face interaction with professors and peers.

(A) opposing to
(B) to oppose to
(C) to be opposed
(D) are opposed to

中譯 **(D)** 另一方面，最近的線上課程調查顯示，900 位大學生中，有 65% 的人表示，因為沒有面對面和教授與同儕互動，他們仍然反對取消校園實體課程。

解析 本題屬於『被動式』中「oppose」的被動考法。由前面結構（主詞）判斷，後面的動詞變化應該用被動式 (beV + V-p.p.)；又由上下文的句意判斷，應當用「介系詞 (to)」，中文翻成「反對……」。所以答案選 (D)。

超語感練習 🎧 Track 253

On the other hand in a recent survey on online classes, 65% of 900 university students said they still are opposed to no on-campus classes, because of the face to face interaction with professors and peers.

14. Online Cloud offers a cheap way of transmitting data, but one may - - - - - - - - whether the costs of doing any data downloads through the Internet have been estimated correctly.

(A) be puzzled
(B) puzzle
(C) be puzzling
(D) have puzzled

中譯 (A) 線上雲端提供了一種傳輸數據的廉價方式；然而，令人困惑的是，透過網路所做的資料下載，其成本是否一直以來被正確地估計。

解析 本題屬於『被動式』中「情緒動詞 (puzzle)」的被動考法。由前面結構（主詞）與句意判斷，後面的動詞變化應該用被動式 (beV + V-p.p.)，中文翻成「使人困惑的……」。所以答案選 (A)。

超語感練習  Track 254

Online Cloud offers a cheap way of transmitting data, but one may be puzzled whether the costs of doing any data downloads through the Internet have been estimated correctly.

15. Our regular customers will - - - - - - - - closely viewing their past ordering record and individual pricing information via the new online order processing system, cumulated in the big data.

(A) absorb in

(B) be absorbed in

(C) be absorbing in

(D) absorb

中譯 (B) 透過累積於大數據的新網上訂單處理系統，我們的熟客將緊密地專注觀察自己的過去訂貨記錄，和個別訂價的信息。

解析 本題屬於『被動式』中「absorb」的被動考法。由前面結構（助動詞 will）與句意判斷，後面的動詞變化應該用被動式 (beV + V-p.p.)；又由上下文的句意判斷，應當用「介系詞 (in)」，中文翻成「專注於……；致力於……」。所以答案選 (B)。

超語感練習 **Track 255**

Our regular customers will be absorbed in closely viewing their past ordering record and individual pricing information via the new online order processing system, cumulated in the big data.

16. Perfect computer networking management system, rich manufacturing and outstanding production techniques make our company - - - - - - - - to our competitors in jewelry industry.

(A) be advanced
(B) advanced
(C) to be advanced
(D) to advance

中譯 (B) 完善的電腦網絡管理系統、大量的製造和優秀的生產技術，使我們在珠寶業領先我們的競爭對手。

解析 本題屬於『被動式』中「使役動詞 (make)」的被動考法。由前面結構（受詞）與句意判斷，後面的動詞變化應該用被動式 (V-p.p.) 當作「形容詞」用，中文翻成「進步的」。所以答案選 (B)。

超語感練習  Track 256

Perfect computer networking management system, rich manufacturing and outstanding production techniques make our company advanced to our competitors in jewelry industry.

17. The satellite broadband service internet providers offers is
a service that many rural or out of the way areas are not
-------- from their cable company or other providers.
(A) to be offered
(B) offering
(C) offered
(D) to be offering

中譯 (C) 許多農村或化外之地的有線電視公司和其他供應商，並沒有網路供
應商所提供的衛星寬頻服務。

解析 本題屬於『被動式』中「offer」的被動考法。由前面結構（主詞）與句
意判斷，後面的動詞變化應該用被動式 (beV＋V-p.p.)，中文翻成「被
提供……」。所以答案選 (C)。

超語感練習 🎧 Track 257

The satellite broadband service internet providers
offers is a service that many rural or out of the way
areas are not offered from their cable company or
other providers.

18. Please remember that you must choose whether or not the company can share private information with others; otherwise, your private data will - - - - - - - - as the company's continuous practice of selling or sharing with anyone it chooses.

(A) be treated
(B) to treat
(C) to be treated
(D) treated

中譯 **(A)** 請記住，你必須選擇公司是否能與他人共享私人信息；否則，您的私人資料將被公司視為可繼續由公司所出售或分享給任何對象。

解析 本題屬於『被動式』中「treat」的被動考法。由前面結構（助動詞 will）與句意判斷，後面的動詞變化應該用被動式 (beV + V-p.p.)，中文翻成「被當作……」。所以答案選 (A)。

超語感練習 Track 258

Please remember that you must choose whether or not the company can share private information with others; otherwise, your private data will be treated as the company's continuous practice of selling or sharing with anyone it chooses.

19. In this region where plenty of export zones - - - - - - -,
thanks to the state-of-the-art production methods, the smart
TVs can be largely produced before the deadline to meet
customers' expectations.

(A) be situated

(B) are situated

(C) to be situated

(D) situated

中譯　(B) 由於先進的生產方式，位於此區域內的許多出口加工區，可以在最
後期限前，大量地製造智能電視，以滿足客戶的期望。

解析　本題屬於『被動式』中 "situate" 的被動考法。由前面結構（主詞）
與句意判斷，後面的動詞變化應該用被動式 (beV + V-p.p.)，中文翻成
「座落於……」。所以答案選 (B)。

超語感練習　🎧 Track 259

In this region where plenty of export zones are
situated, thanks to the state-of-the-art production
methods, the smart TVs can be largely produced
before the deadline to meet customers' expectations.

20. The demand of our bio-chemical products in weight-losing has grown exponentially, and with that, of course, the need for more orders ---------.

(A) demanded
(B) is demanded
(C) is being demanded
(D) is demanding

中譯 **(B)** 在我們減重的生物化工產品上，需求成倍數增長，因此，會有更多訂單的需求。

解析 本題屬於『被動式』中 "demand" 的被動考法。由前面結構（主詞）與句意判斷，後面的動詞變化應該用被動式 (beV + V-p.p.)，中文翻成「被要求」。所以答案選 (B)。

超語感練習 Track 260

The demand of our bio-chemical products in weight-losing has grown exponentially, and with that, of course, the need for more orders is demanded.

21. The price and performance gaps between notebook PCs and desktops are narrowing due to the continuous improvements - - - - - - - - reducing prices in notebook PC components and costs in promotion.

(A) made up of
(B) makes up
(C) are making up
(D) are made

中譯　(A) 因為筆記本電腦組件價格、和宣傳成本降低的不斷改進之下，筆記型電腦和桌上型電腦在價格和性能之間的差距正在縮小。

解析　本題屬於『被動式』中 "make" 的被動考法。由前面結構（主詞）判斷，後面的動詞變化應該用被動式 (beV + V-p.p.)；又由上下文的句意判斷，應當用「介系詞 (up + of)」，中文翻成「由……所組成」。所以答案選 (A)。

超語感練習　🎧 Track 261

The price and performance gaps between notebook PCs and desktops are narrowing due to the continuous improvements made up of reducing prices in notebook PC components and costs in promotion.

22. The database security has been critically improved, going well past encryption and passwords, and now - - - - - - - - employing a range of access control features plus digital signatures.

(A) are known for
(B) known as
(C) to be known to
(D) know as

中譯　(A) 資料庫安全已大大地被改善，且適用過去的加密系統和密碼，而現在廣為人知的，是採用了一系列的控制特徵，加上數位化的簽名。

解析　本題屬於『被動式』中 "know" 的被動考法。由前面結構（主詞）判斷，後面的動詞變化應該用被動式 (beV + V-p.p.)；又由上下文的句意判斷，應當用「介系詞 (for)」，中文翻成「因……而廣為人知」。所以答案選 (A)。

超語感練習　🎧 Track 262

The database security has been critically improved, going well past encryption and passwords, and now are known for employing a range of access control features plus digital signatures.

23. The forecast concerning telecommunications, networking equipment and services market has - - - - - - - significantly downward in the face of further negative market.

(A) be revised
(B) to revise
(C) to be revised
(D) been revised

中譯 (D) 關於電信、網絡設備和服務市場的預測，在面對更進一步的市場負面影響之下，已經顯著往下修訂。

解析 本題屬於『被動式』中「revise」的被動考法。由前面結構（助動詞 has）句意判斷，後面的動詞變化應該用完成式的被動 (have/has been ＋ V-p.p.)，中文翻成「被修正」。所以答案選 (D)。

超語感練習 🎧 Track 263

The forecast concerning telecommunications, networking equipment and services market has been revised significantly downward in the face of further negative market.

24. While the traditional class teaching is - - - - - - - - the popularity of online classes, which does not mean that on-campus classes will become a thing of the past.

(A) being replacing with
(B) replaced with
(C) to be replaced with
(D) being replaced with

中譯 (D) 而正當傳統的課堂教學正漸漸被線上課程的普及所替換時，這並不表示在學校上課將會成為歷史。

解析 本題屬於『被動式』中「replace」的被動考法。由前面結構（動詞）句意判斷，後面的動詞變化應該用被動式 (beV + V-p.p. + with)；又由上下文的句意判斷，應當用「進行式 (being)」，中文翻成「逐漸變成被取代……」。所以答案選 (D)。

超語感練習 Track 264

While the traditional class teaching is being replaced with the popularity of online classes, which does not mean that on-campus classes will become a thing of the past.

25. Many of the country's oldest - - - - - - - - have fallen into disrepair due to the lack of government funding.

(A) people
(B) services
(C) monuments
(D) rivers

中譯 (C) 許多國家最古老的遺跡年久失修倒塌，是由於政府資金匱乏。

解析 此題為單字題，選項 (A) 為人、選項 (B) 為服務、選項 (D) 為河，依題意應選擇 (C) 遺址，最為恰當。

超語感練習 🎧 Track 265

Many of the country's oldest monuments have fallen into disrepair due to the lack of government funding.

26. Recent increases in the price of oil have been - - - - - - - - reflected by prices at the pumps at gas stations.
   (A) quickly
   (B) quick
   (C) quickness
   (D) quicken

中譯 (A) 近來原油上漲，已經很快地反映在加油站加油箱上頭顯示的價格上了。

解析 必須選擇副詞，因為只有副詞能修飾過去分詞 reflected。(B)quick「快的」是形容詞。(C)quickness「迅速」是名詞。(D)quicken「加快」是動詞。

超語感練習 🎧 Track 266

Recent increases in the price of oil have been quickly reflected by prices at the pumps at gas stations.

27. After many trials, we have found replacement equipment that seems - - - - - - - -.

(A) acceptable
(B) to accept
(C) accept
(D) acceptably

中譯 (A) 在許多試用之後,我們找到了似乎可以接受的替換設備。

解析 seem「似乎」是連綴動詞。連綴動詞後是主詞補語。主詞補語可以是形容詞故答案為 (A)acceptable「可接受的」。(B)to accept「接受」是不定詞,(C)accept「接受」是動詞。(D)acceptably「可接受地」是副詞。

超語感練習 🎧 Track 267

After many trials, we have found replacement equipment that seems acceptable.

28. The increased popularity of car ownership in China has placed a great strain on its road - - - - - - - -.
(A) surface
(B) web
(C) network
(D) lines

中譯　(C) 中國擁有車子的人口增加，已造成整個道路系統上的一大負擔。

解析　此題為單字題，選項 (A) 為表面、選項 (B) 為網、選項 (D) 為線，依題意應選擇 (C) 系統，最為恰當。

超語感練習　Track 268

The increased popularity of car ownership in China has placed a great strain on its road network.

29. We have been informed that service will be - - - - - - - - as soon as the fault has been repaired.

(A) resume
(B) resuming
(C) resumed
(D) resumes

中譯　(C) 我們被告知一旦問題修復好，就會馬上恢復服務。

解析　未來式被動語態，主詞＋ will be ＋過去分詞，故選 (C)。例句：Wendy will be a superstar in ten years.（Wendy 十年後將會是超級明星。）

超語感練習　Track 269

We have been informed that service will be resumed as soon as the fault has been repaired.

30. Television is often used by parents to keep their children -------- when they are busy.

(A) entertained
(B) entertaining
(C) entertain
(D) entertainingly

中譯 (A) 電視常被父母當做是在他們忙碌的時候，娛樂孩子們的工具。

解析 以過去分詞作形容詞，當受詞補語，修飾 "their children"「他們的小孩」，故選擇選項 (A)。選項 (B) 為現在分詞、選項 (C) 為動詞、選項 (D) 為副詞。

超語感練習 Track 270

Television is often used by parents to keep their children entertained when they are busy.

擬真試題

1. Each forum will have essentially the same agenda, - - - - - - - - you are invited to attend the one most convenient to your location and schedule.

(A) which
(B) who
(C) but
(D) and

中譯 (D) 每個座談會都有基本相同的議程邀請您按照您最方便的地點和時間表參加。

解析 本題考題屬於『連接詞』中,「對等子句」的考法。由上下文判斷,空格後面是「句子」的結構,為「完整句意」,所以答案選 (D)。因為句意沒有前後相反,所以選項 (C) 不考慮。

超語感練習 Track 271

Each forum will have essentially the same agenda, and you are invited to attend the one most convenient to your location and schedule.

2. Our industry must contend with a growing number of companies; - - - - - - - - aggressively launch popular models in the market.

(A) which

(B) that

(C) because

(D) who

中譯 (A) 我們的行業必須與越來越多、積極推出且受市場歡迎產品的公司競爭。

解析 本題考題屬於『連接詞』中,「形容詞子句」的考法。由上下文判斷,空格後面是「動詞」,為「不完整句意」,又連接 2 個句子,所以空格為「連接詞」功能的「形容詞子句」用法;又前面有逗點存在,是屬於「非限定用法」,所以先排除答案 (B)。前面「先行詞」又為「非人」的對象,所以答案選 (A)。

超語感練習  Track 272

Our industry must contend with a growing number of companies; which aggressively launch popular models in the market.

Unit 10

3. Successful companies find ways to gather accurate information, and make the best use of it, - - - - - - - makes the companies worth their salt.

(A) who
(B) that
(C) because
(D) which

中譯 **(D)** 成功的企業找出收集準確信息的辦法，並充分利用它，使之實至名歸。

解析 本題考題屬於『連接詞』中，「形容詞子句」的考法。由上下文判斷，空格後面是「動詞」，為「不完整句意」，又連接 2 個句子，所以空格為「連接詞」功能的「形容詞子句」用法；又前面有逗點存在，是屬於「非限定用法」，所以先排除答案 (B)。前面「先行詞」又為「非人」的對象，所以排除答案 (A)；所以答案選 (D)。

超語感練習 Track 273

Successful companies find ways to gather accurate information, and make the best use of it, which makes the companies worth their salt.

4. - - - - - - - - it is carefully designed and administered, a flextime program will provide significant benefits to mutual interests and trust between the firm and employees.

(A) Despite
(B) Though
(C) When
(D) As soon as

中譯 (C) 當精心設計和管理時，彈性工時計劃將為雙方的共同利益和信任，提供重要的好處。

解析 本題考題屬於『連接詞』中，「副詞子句」的考法。選項 (D) 中文翻譯為「一⋯就⋯⋯」，表示動作一前一後緊接著發生，與句意不符，所以不選。由上下文判斷，空格後面是「副詞」功能的子句用法，所以空格所在句子的結構應該是「副詞子句」，表示「時間」的「當⋯⋯時候」，所以答案選 (C)。

超語感練習  Track 274

When it is carefully designed and administered, a flextime program will provide significant benefits to mutual interests and trust between the firm and employees.

5. Please email your name, mailing address, fax number and e-mail address - - - - - - - - are reachable, to the Head Office at your earliest convenience.

(A) that
(B) who
(C) despite
(D) where

中譯 (A) 請在您儘早以 e-mail 發送您的姓名、郵寄地址、傳真號碼及電子郵件地址至總公司。

解析 本題考題屬於『連接詞』中,「形容詞子句」的考法。由上下文判斷,空格後面是「動詞」,為「不完整句意」,又連接 2 個句子,所以空格為「連接詞」功能的「形容詞子句」用法。前面「先行詞」又為「非人」的對象,所以排除表示「地方」的答案 (D) 與表示「人」的答案 (B);答案 (C) 為介系詞,所以不選。所以答案選 (A)。

超語感練習 🎧 Track 275

Please email your name, mailing address, fax number and e-mail address that are reachable, to the Head Office at your earliest convenience.

6. We visited the Port of Vancouver, - - - - - - - - is noted for its successful transition to modern facilities, and its environmental protection.

(A) who
(B) because
(C) which
(D) that

中譯 (C) 我們參觀溫哥華港，而這地方是因為成功轉型為現代化的設施、對環境的保護而聞名。

解析 本題考題屬於『連接詞』中，「形容詞子句」的考法。由上下文判斷，空格後面是「動詞」，為「不完整句意」，又連接 2 個句子，所以空格為「連接詞」功能的「形容詞子句」用法；又前面有逗點存在，是屬於「非限定用法」，所以先排除答案 (D)。前面「先行詞」又為「非人」的對象，所以排除答案 (A)；所以答案選 (C)。

超語感練習  Track 276

We visited the Port of Vancouver, which is noted for its successful transition to modern facilities, and its environmental protection.

7. -------- talking during the video conference with potential buyers, you need to be sure to speak clearly and not too fast.

(A) As soon as
(B) Though
(C) Before
(D) When

中譯 (D) 當你用視訊會議與可能的買家商談時，你需要確認講清楚，不要太快。

解析 本題考題屬於『連接詞』中，「副詞子句」的考法。由上下文判斷，空格後面是省略主詞所形成的「現在分詞」，因為空格所在的句子為副詞功能的子句用法，表示「時間」的「當……時候」，而後面結構是「主要子句」所以答案選 (D)。

超語感練習 🎧 Track 277

When talking during the video conference with potential buyers, you need to be sure to speak clearly and not too fast.

8. A merger will actually allow us to serve our customers even better, -------- the service areas and resources of each company will be combined into one.

(A) because
(B) though
(C) before
(D) when

超語感練習 Track 278

A merger will actually allow us to serve our customers even better, because the service areas and resources of each company will be combined into one.

9. Both of our companies - - - - - - - - have established a solid reputation for providing great service and options for our customers are competitive in providing reasonable prices.

(A) who
(B) because
(C) so
(D) that

中譯 (D) 在提供我們的客戶，卓越的服務與選擇方面，已建立良好聲譽的我方兩家公司，在提供合理的價格方面，是相當具有競爭力的。

解析 本題考題屬於『連接詞』中，「形容詞子句」的考法。由上下文判斷，空格後面是「動詞」，為「不完整句意」，又連接 2 個句子，所以空格為「連接詞」功能的「形容詞子句」用法；前面「先行詞」又為「非人」的對象，所以排除答案 (A)；所以答案選 (D)。

超語感練習 🎧 Track 279

Both of our companies that have established a solid reputation for providing great service and options for our customers are competitive in providing reasonable prices.

10. Regular checking customers - - - - - - - - prefer to maintain a lower checking balance to avoid monthly maintenance fees will enjoy this non-interest bearing account with unlimited check writing.

(A) which

(B) because

(C) who

(D) what

中譯 (C) 偏好維持較低的支票餘額，以避免每月維護費的定期支票客戶，將享有這無息帳戶、無限的支票開立使用。

解析 本題考題屬於『連接詞』中，「形容詞子句」的考法。由上下文判斷，空格後面是「動詞」，為「不完整句意」，又連接 2 個句子，所以空格為「連接詞」功能的「形容詞子句」用法。前面「先行詞」又為「人」的對象，所以排除答案 (A)；選項 (D) what 前面不需要名詞，所以排除。所以答案選 (C)。

超語感練習 Track 280

Regular checking customers who prefer to maintain a lower checking balance to avoid monthly maintenance fees will enjoy this non-interest bearing account with unlimited check writing.

11. It proves to be real - - - - - - - - depression in Asia, falling exports, declining corporate profits and stagnant wages could be the cause of slowing spending and curbing economic growth.

(A) though
(B) despite
(C) that
(D) who

中譯　(C) 亞洲的經濟蕭條、出口下降、企業利潤不斷下降和停滯的工資，可能成為消費遲緩、遏制經濟增長的原因，這件事，已被證明是真的。

解析　本題考題屬於『連接詞』中，「名詞子句」的考法。由上下文判斷，空格後面是「完整句意」，所以空格為「連接詞」功能的「名詞子句」用法。所以答案選 (C)。

超語感練習　🎧 Track 281

It proves to be real that depression in Asia, falling exports, declining corporate profits and stagnant wages could be the cause of slowing spending and curbing economic growth.

12. Our Global Market Expansion Project draft would have been completed by the end of last month - - - - - - - all of the related tasks had been distributed equally.

(A) providing
(B) though
(C) after
(D) while

中譯　(A) 假如所有相關的任務平均地被分配的話，我們的全球市場擴張計劃草案將已經於上個月月底完成。

解析　本題考題屬於『連接詞』中，「副詞子句」的考法。由上下文判斷，空格所在的句子為「副詞」功能的子句用法，表示「假設」的「如果⋯⋯」，而前面結構是「主要子句」，所以答案選 (A)。

超語感練習 Track 282

Our Global Market Expansion Project draft would have been completed by the end of last month providing all of the related tasks had been distributed equally.

13. The quarterly reports indicate the number of our product enquiries from the United States has decreased slightly in recent years - - - - - - - - the numbers of Japanese and European consumers grew.

(A) because of
(B) though
(C) while
(D) where

中譯 (C) 季報告指出，在美國，我們產品詢問度的數字，在近幾年略有下降，而日本和歐洲的消費者人數卻有增長。

解析 本題考題屬於『連接詞』中，「副詞子句」的考法。由上下文判斷，因為空格所在的句子為副詞功能的子句用法，表示「對比、對照」的「雖然、儘管」，而前面結構是「主要子句」所以答案選 (C)。

超語感練習 🎧 Track 283

The quarterly reports indicate the number of our product enquiries from the United States has decreased slightly in recent years while the numbers of Japanese and European consumers grew.

14. Diners are admonished that smoking - - - - - - - - in designated smoking areas only, available in certain restaurants and airports.

(A) to have been permitted
(B) to be permitted
(C) permitted
(D) be permitted

中譯 (D) 用餐者被告誡，吸煙只能在某些餐館和機場所唯一指定的、可被允許的吸煙區。

解析 本題考題屬於『意志動詞』的考法。由句中連接詞 (that) 與動詞 (admonished) 判斷，空格的動詞應當用省略「助動詞 (should)」之後的「動詞原形 (VR)」；又由上下句意判斷，應該要用「被動」，所以答案選 (D)。

超語感練習 Track 284

Diners are admonished that smoking be permitted in designated smoking areas only, available in certain restaurants and airports.

15. - - - - - - - the reservations staff notified the clients, the additional information would have become needed to complete their requests.

(A) If
(B) Had
(C) Should
(D) Were

(B) 假如預約公司的工作人員通知客戶的話，完成他們要求便需要這份額外的資料。

本題考題屬於『假設語氣』考法中，「連接詞的省略」，且與「過去時間」相反的假設。本句的答案首先去除 (C)，因為「助動詞」後面應該接「動詞原形 (VR)」，與題目不合。又由上下句意判斷，本句應該用「主動」，所以又排除 (D)。由後面的動詞 (notified) 與動詞 (would have become) 判斷，空格的動詞應當用省略「連接詞 (if)」之後，選擇用「助動詞」往前挪動的「完成式助動詞 (had)」(If the reservations staff had notified the clients)，所以答案選 (B)。

超語感練習 🎧 Track 285

Had the reservations staff notified the clients, the additional information would have become needed to complete their requests.

16. If I - - - - - - - - with the professional yet friendly atmosphere in your office, it would prove your effort in rebuilding the branch.

(A) was impressed
(B) impressed
(C) were impressed
(D) had impressed

中譯 (C) 如果我對你辦公室專業、友好的氣氛留下深刻的印象，那就證明，你於重建分公司的努力。

解析 本題考題屬於『假設語氣』考法中，與「現在時間」相反的假設。由句中連接詞 (if) 與動詞 (would prove) 判斷，空格的動詞應當用與「現在時間」相反的「過去式」；但是因為是「附屬子句」，不需要「助動詞」，又由上下句意判斷，應該要用「被動式」，所以答案選 (C)。

超語感練習 Track 286

If I were impressed with the professional yet friendly atmosphere in your office, it would prove your effort in rebuilding the branch.

17. It is imperative that our company - - - - - - - - our customers with a gratifying travel experience, and thus, we would like your positive feedback on your trip.

(A) should have provided

(B) provided

(C) provides

(D) provide

中譯 (D) 重要的是，本公司為客戶提供了令人滿意的旅行體驗，因此，我們希望來自於您旅途中的正面回饋。

解析 本題考題屬於『意志形容詞』的考法。由句中連接詞 (that) 與形容詞 (imperative) 判斷，空格的動詞應當用省略「助動詞 (should)」之後的「動詞原形 (VR)」；又由上下句意判斷，應該要用「主動」，所以答案選 (D)。

超語感練習 🎧 Track 287

It is imperative that our company provide our customers with a gratifying travel experience, and thus, we would like your positive feedback on your trip.

18. It is recommended that passengers - - - - - - - in at the desk at least 1 hour prior to their scheduled departure time.

(A) should be checked
(B) should check
(C) checked
(D) be checked

中譯　(B) 我們建議乘客，至少應在他們的預定起飛時間 1 個小時前，在臨櫃辦理入境手續。

解析　本題考題屬於『意志動詞』的考法。由句中連接詞 (that) 與動詞 (recommended) 判斷，空格的動詞應當用「助動詞 (should)」之後的「動詞原形 (VR)」；又由上下句意判斷，應該要用「主動」，所以答案選 (B)。

超語感練習　🎧 Track 288

It is recommended that passengers should check in at the desk at least 1 hour prior to their scheduled departure time.

19. We are in hope that this situation of schedule delay
-------- on account of simple oversight or clerical error.
(A) were not to take place
(B) have not taken place
(C) take place
(D) would not take place

中譯 (D) 我們希望，不要因為小疏忽或筆誤，而發生行程延遲這種情況。

解析 本題考題屬於『假設語氣』考法中，「希望」的用法。由句中連接詞
(that) 與動詞 (is) 判斷，in a hope 後面句意為假，整個時間又是「現在
時間」，空格的動詞應當用與「現在時間」相反的「過去式」，且為「主
動、否定」用法，所以答案選 (D)。

超語感練習 🎧 Track 289

We are in hope that this situation of schedule delay
would not take place on account of simple oversight
or clerical error.

20. - - - - - - - - you have technical problems with our online ticket system, you could contact the Technical Desk at (886) 523-4642.

(A) If
(B) Should
(C) Had
(D) Were

中譯 **(B)** 如果您對我們的線上售票系統，有技術上的問題，您可以聯繫技術服務台，電話是 (886) 523-4642。

解析 本題考題屬於『假設語氣』考法中，「連接詞的省略」與「未來時間」相反、「萬一」發生的假設。首先排除選項(A)，因為前後動詞時態不一致；由後面的動詞 (have) 為動詞原形，與動詞 (could contact) 判斷，空格應當用省略「連接詞(if)」之後，「助動詞」往前挪動的「助動詞(Should)」。本句的答案選(B)，因為「助動詞」後面應該接「動詞原形(VR)」。

超語感練習 Track 290

Should you have technical problems with our online ticket system, you could contact the Technical Desk at (886) 523-4642.

21. - - - - - - - - it at the commendation of the mutual-aid organization, a completely independent agency would be established to investigate passengers' complaints against airlines and other related personnel.

(A) If
(B) Should
(C) Were
(D) Had

中譯 (C) 萬一這件事經互助機構表揚，那麼就要設立一個完全獨立的機構，針對乘客對航空公司和其他相關人員的投訴進行調查。

解析 本題考題屬於『假設語氣』考法中，「連接詞的省略」，且與「現在時間」相反的假設。本句由上下句意判斷，2 個句子應當要有 1 個連接詞；然而前面結構缺少動詞，後面的動詞 (would be) 為「過去式」，為「主要子句」。所以判斷空格應當使用「動詞」，為「省略連接詞」的句型。句意判斷應當用「beV」，所以答案選 (C)。

超語感練習 🎧 Track 291

Were it at the commendation of the mutual-aid organization, a completely independent agency would be established to investigate passengers' complaints against airlines and other related personnel.

22. The real estate expert advised Jack that he - - - - - - - - renegotiating with the local agency after he noticed some problems with the accommodations.

(A) should be considered
(B) should consider
(C) consider
(D) be considered

中譯 (C) 房地產專家建議，Jack 應在發現一些住宿的問題之後，考慮當地的代理機構重新協商。

解析 本題考題屬於『意志動詞』的考法。由句中連接詞(that)與動詞(advised)判斷，空格的動詞應當用「助動詞(should)」之後的「動詞原形(VR)」；又由上下句意判斷，應該要用「主動」，所以答案選(C)。

超語感練習  Track 292

The real estate expert advised Jack that he consider renegotiating with the local agency after he noticed some problems with the accommodations.

Unit 10

23. Under the rental policy, the boss declared as if Robert, the leaseholder - - - - - - - - fully responsible for the possible equipment damage.

(A) had been
(B) was to be
(C) were to be
(D) has been

中譯 (A) 根據租賃條約，老闆宣稱，租賃者 Robert 似乎要完全擔負可能的設備損壞。

解析 本題考題屬於『假設語氣』考法中，「彷彿、好像」的連接詞用法。由句中連接詞 (as if) 與動詞 (declared) 判斷，as if 後面句意為假，整個時間又是「過去時間」，空格的動詞應當用與「過去時間」相反的「過去完成式」，所以答案選 (A)。

超語感練習 🎧 Track 293

Under the rental policy, the boss declared as if Robert, the leaseholder had been fully responsible for the possible equipment damage.

24. If we wanted to find something different, today's net world --------- it accessible to find new, even much cheaper air-line tickets to streamline our expenses.

(A) made
(B) would make
(C) would have made
(D) had made

中譯 (B) 如果我們想有不同的選擇，今日的網路世界，讓我們得以找到新的、甚至是更便宜的廉價機票，以節省我們的開銷。

解析 本題考題屬於『假設語氣』考法中，與「現在時間」相反的假設。由句中連接詞 (if) 與動詞 (wanted) 判斷，空格的動詞應當用與「現在時間」相反的「過去式」；但是因為是「主要子句」，需要「助動詞 (would)」，又由上下句意判斷，應該要用「主動」，所以答案選 (B)。

超語感練習 Track 294

If we wanted to find something different, today's net world would make it accessible to find new, even much cheaper air-line tickets to streamline our expenses.

25. Nelson, one of the oldest cities in the UK, is highly suggested that it - - - - - - - - a renewal of its urban center by the use of appropriate technologies and knowledge for better environment and quality of life.

(A) have to be carried out

(B) have carried out

(C) to carry out

(D) should carry out

中譯 (A) Nelson，英國最古老的城市之一，強烈地被建議，為更好的環境和生活品質，必須藉由使用適當的技術和知識，對其市中心進行更新。

解析 本題考題屬於『意志動詞』的考法。由句中連接詞 (that) 與動詞 (is suggest) 判斷，空格的動詞應當用「助動詞 (should)」加上「動詞原形 (VR)」；又由上下句意判斷，應該要用「被動」，所以答案選 (A)。

超語感練習　🎧 Track 295

Nelson, one of the oldest cities in the UK, is highly suggested that it have to be carried out a renewal of its urban center by the use of appropriate technologies and knowledge for better environment and quality of life.

26. But that the company promised to customize the touring routes either from a functional standpoint or from a security standpoint, the specific needs of your organization - - - - - - - -.
(A) could not have been met
(B) could have been met
(C) could be met
(D) have not been met

中譯 (A) 若不是該公司從功能的角度或安全的角度承諾去制式化旅遊路線，您公司的特定需求將無法達成。

解析 本題考題屬於『假設語氣』考法中，「若非、要不是」的用法。由句中連接詞 (but that) 與動詞 (promised) 判斷，but that 後面句意為真，主要子句為假，整個時間又是「過去時間」，空格的動詞應當用與「過去時間」相反的「過去式助動詞 (could) ＋完成式」，且為情緒動詞「被動、否定」用法，所以答案選 (A)。

超語感練習 Track 296

But that the company promised to customize the touring routes either from a functional standpoint or from a security standpoint, the specific needs of your organization could not have been met.

27. If you need one-on-one consulting service on route planning, I - - - - - - - - available to meet with you at any time from 2 o'clock onwards because I'm out of the office until then.

(A) were
(B) would have been
(C) should
(D) will be

中譯　(D) 如果您在路線規劃上，需要一對一的諮詢服務，我要到2點後，才有空為您服務；因為在那時前，我都不在辦公室。

解析　本題考題屬於『假設語氣』考法中，與「未來時間」相反、「直說法」的假設。由句中連接詞 (if) 與動詞 (need) 判斷，空格的動詞應當用「未來式」；因為是「主要子句」，需要使用「助動詞」，所以答案選 (D)。

超語感練習　Track 297

If you need one-on-one consulting service on route planning, I will be available to meet with you at any time from 2 o'clock onwards because I'm out of the office until then.

28. On account of the rapid shuttle bus, distances from most London theaters to a huge array of famous restaurants, pubs, clubs, and shops - - - - - - - - as if it were within a ten-minute walk.

(A) are shortened

(B) have been shortened

(C) have shortened

(D) were shortened

中譯 (A) 因為快速的接駁巴士，從大多數倫敦的劇院，到一系列著名的餐廳、酒吧、夜總會和商店的距離，縮短到好像在 10 分鐘之內的步行路程一樣。

解析 本題考題屬於『假設語氣』考法中，「彷彿、好像」的連接詞用法。由句中連接詞 (as if) 與動詞 (were) 判斷，as if 後面句意為假，整個時間又是「現在時間」，空格的動詞應當用與「現在時間」的事實，用「現在式」，又為「被動」，所以答案選 (A)。

超語感練習 Track 298

On account of the rapid shuttle bus, distances from most London theaters to a huge array of famous restaurants, pubs, clubs and shops are shortened as if it were within a ten-minute walk.

29. - - - - - - - - the airline have expanded its cargo operations substantially, its new cargo routes will open, and the flight frequency on its existing cargo routes will increase.

(A) If
(B) Were
(C) Should
(D) Had

中譯 (C) 如果航空公司已大大擴張其貨運業務,那麼它的貨運航線將開放, 而現行貨運航線的頻繁次數將會增加。

解析 本題考題屬於『假設語氣』考法中,「連接詞的省略」,且與「未來時間」相反的假設,「萬一」發生的假設。選項 (B)、(C) 優先排除,因為後面都必須接「過去分詞 (V-p.p.)」結構;與文法不符,所以不選。本句由上下句意判斷,2 個句子應當要有 1 個連接詞;然而前面結構為動詞原形 (VR) 的 have + V-p.p.,後面「主要子句」的動詞 (will open) 為「未來式」。所以判斷空格應當使用「動詞」,為「省略連接詞」的句型。句意判斷應當用「should」,所以答案選 (C)。

超語感練習 🎧 **Track 299**

Should the airline have expanded its cargo operations substantially, its new cargo routes will open, and the flight frequency on its existing cargo routes will increase.

30. Results from a recent survey indicate that suppose an illness - - - - - - - - contagious, nearly half of Americans would be so concerned about catching a fellow passenger's illness that they would ask to be reseated.

(A) were reported
(B) would be made
(C) would have reported
(D) were to report

中譯 **(A)** 從最近的一項調查結果顯示，假設疾病被報導具有傳染性，會有將近一半的美國人因擔心染上同行乘客的病，而要求重新安排座位。

解析 本題考題屬於『假設語氣』考法中，與「現在時間」相反的假設。由句中連接詞 (suppose) 與動詞 (would be... concerned) 判斷，空格的動詞應當用與「現在時間」相反的「過去式」；但是因為是「附屬子句」，又由上下句意判斷，應該要用「被動」，所以答案選 (A)。

超語感練習 Track 300

Results from a recent survey indicate that suppose an illness were reported contagious, nearly half of Americans would be so concerned about catching a fellow passenger's illness that they would ask to be reseated.

Leader 016

聽新多益 Part 5，第一次就拿閱讀高分

作　　者　力得文化編輯群
封面構成　高鍾琪
內頁構成　華漢電腦排版有限公司

發 行 人　周瑞德
企劃編輯　陳欣慧
校　　對　陳韋佑、饒美君
印　　製　大亞彩色印刷製版股份有限公司
初　　版　2015 年 4 月
定　　價　新台幣 369 元
出　　版　力得文化
電　　話　(02) 2351-2007
傳　　真　(02) 2351-0887
地　　址　100 台北市中正區福州街 1 號 10 樓之 2
E - m a i l　best.books.service@gmail.com

港澳地區總經銷　泛華發行代理有限公司
地　　　　址　香港新界將軍澳工業邨駿昌街 7 號 2 樓
電　　　　話　(852) 2798-2323
傳　　　　真　(852) 2796-5471

國家圖書館出版品預行編目(CIP)資料

聽新多益 Part 5,第一次就拿閱讀高分 / 力得文
化編輯群著. -- 初版. -- 臺北市 : 力得文化,
2015.04
　面　；　公分. -- (Leader ; 16)
ISBN 978-986-91458-5-5(平裝附光碟片）

1. 多益測驗

805.1895　　　　　　　　104004916